HER BROKEN TRUST

A ROSEMARY RUN THRILLER

KELLY UTT

PROLOGUE

Layla Grant was angry. Urgently, desperately angry.

Her blood boiled inside her veins. She could feel it sloshing around her body, hot and insistent. If she didn't know better, she'd have thought steam was rising from her ears on a regular basis as well.

She'd tried literally every possible way to stuff her anger down, to wish it away, to numb it, to drown it with alcohol, and even to take it out on others who might help shoulder the burden.

Nothing had worked. She'd remained imprisoned by her rage.

It seemed there was no escape. Not for Layla or for her husband, Trent Grant, who had been convicted of serious federal charges that could land him in prison for up to thirty years. Not to mention, he could be fined as much as one million dollars. Those facts only stoked the fires of Layla's anger ever further, her organs feeling like molten lava that would soon melt and burn her from the inside out.

She smoothed her bottle-blonde hair nervously with her manicured pink fingernails as she waited with the crowd that had gathered in the courtroom for Trent's sentencing. People scurried down the main walkway to find a seat on one of the crowded wooden benches, hoping to get settled into a spot before the room was called to order.

A jury had found Trent guilty of bank fraud just two days earlier, and the judicial system had seemed keen to dole out the broken man's punishment as soon as humanly possible.

Despite Layla's wish for space and privacy, a balding old man in a tweed jacket sat down beside her. She gave him a quick smile, but wasn't in any frame of mind to chat. She was afraid that if she opened her mouth to speak to the man, her vitriol would spill out. So, she kept her gaze facing forward, focusing on the back of her husband's head as she tapped a fingertip nervously on one knee.

Tears stung at Layla's eyes. She tried desperately to force them away.

She could usually hide her emotions. She'd had years of practice in pretending that everything was alright. Appearances were important, after all. Especially in Rosemary Run, where every family seemed to have a perfect life.

Layla hoped she could hold it together for the entirety of the proceedings. She had been warned that a dramatic display of emotion could irritate the judge and make him come down harder on Trent as a result.

Once things got started, time moved at what felt like warp speed, everything set on fast forward. The crowd stood as Judge Roger Trumbell entered, then flattened his silky black robe, got comfortable behind the bench, and pounded his gavel. When he was finished, the people in the courtroom went back down as shuffling and nervous energy permeated the space.

There had been a lot of media interest in Trent's case. Judge Trumbell had barred members of the media from entering the courtroom, but a gaggle of reporters and cameramen waited anxiously outside to report on today's outcome the minute they received the news.

Just a short time prior, no one in Rosemary Run had known about the charges. Trent had known longer, and Layla had worked earnestly to keep word from getting out. But like a beachball stuffed under the surface of water, there would be no hiding the truth. Just as that beachball would eventually bounce upward, forcing its way out and into the open air, the truth of the Grant family's predicament had found its way into the light of day.

So far, townspeople had-- *mostly*-- been kind. They'd kept their comments to themselves, at least, long enough for Layla and the kids to keep from hearing them as they'd navigated grocery store aisles and dinners out. Layla was thankful for that much. It had probably helped that one of Trent's co-workers at the bank, Moe Griffith, was facing similar charges as an alleged co-conspirator.

Moe was a former NFL football player, making the pending charges against him all the more scandalous. His fame took some of the heat off of Trent, who was just a regular guy without the shadow of celebrity status hanging over his head. At least, the public believed Trent was a regular guy. No one had uncovered the deeper truth... yet. That revelation would come later.

Layla's palms sweat as she wrung her hands, feeling the hardness of the unforgiving bench beneath her.

Luckily, she could focus on what was happening without having to tend to her two young girls at the same time. Haily and Bethany had taken the day off school and stayed home with Layla's aunt, Tabatha Rhodes, affectionately called Aunt Tabby. Tabby had recently retired from her decades-long job as a school bus driver, and she was happy to find things to fill her newfound free time.

At ages seven and five, the trouble Trent faced was more than the Grant girls could comprehend. In fact, Layla had insisted that no one tell the girls the truth of what was really happening. If Trent did-- *God forbid*-- get sent to prison, Layla would tell the girls that he was away traveling for work. She knew it sounded preposterous because their father's sentence could span decades, but protecting her family was priority number one.

What kind of mother would she be if she didn't shield her young girls from such unpleasant, harsh realities? They needed more time to grow up before learning that their father was a criminal. It would change who they were at a fundamental level. Layla's college degree remained unfinished, but it didn't take book smarts to know how something like this could affect young children.

In a whirlwind of activity, the courtroom participants

followed instructions and routine until it was time for Judge Trumbell to speak the words that would likely change the course of Trent's life forever. Those words would affect his family, too. In a big way.

Layla thought her husband looked weak and frail standing there, bright overhead lights shining hotly on his head of thinning brown hair. He squinted and pursed his lips like a cave-dwelling creature who hadn't seen the light of day in some time.

The stress had taken a toll on Trent and he'd missed one too many workouts. Love handles bulged from his sides. His hunched back made him look easily fifteen-years older. Gone were the muscle tone and physicality of the athletic man Layla had married a decade prior.

Layla felt a pang of guilt as she contemplated Trent, his softness and vulnerability, in part, her fault.

"Does your client wish to say anything before the sentence is imposed?" the judge finally asked, eyeing Trent's council.

Attorney Fred Lowell, a slick, seasoned old man, stood next to Trent at the defendant's table. Fred was known for representing white collar criminals all over Northern California. His track record was good but that didn't mean he was a miracle worker. He had already advised Trent to expect a hefty fine and a significant amount of prison time.

There was no escaping the need to make amends and restitution. In the world of bank fraud, this particular crime had been too heinous to expect any chance of getting off scot-free.

Trent's voice was small and timid, cracking like a teenage boy's as he spoke the words. "No, your honor."

Judge Trumbell spoke quickly, his words booming throughout the room.

"Then I hereby sentence you to a term of twenty-nine years in federal prison and a fine of nine hundred and fifty thousand dollars. Court is adjourned."

The courtroom erupted into a sea of murmurs, gasps, and a few claps upon hearing the news. Someone ran out the back door, presumably to share details with members of the media. Within minutes, Trent's fate would be heard far and wide on TV newscasts and in newspaper articles.

Layla thought she saw her husband's knees buckle, and hers threatened to do the same.

She wanted to scream. Every fiber of her being wanted to wail like a banshee, to let out the frustration and the rage that had consumed her once tranquil existence.

Her fists curled into tight balls. She wanted to pound the marble column in front of her and have it give like bread dough. She wanted the column to bend and bulge inward, taking her pain with it. Her pain needed somewhere to go. If not the column, she wanted to turn and rip the wooden benches from the floor like the Incredible Hulk, busting bolts and loosening screws with ease. She wanted to smash and destroy everything in her sight. She wanted to crush the things around her in the hopes that doing so might dampen the fury pouring from her soul.

But she couldn't.

Countless eyes were on Layla, watching for a reaction, gauging her handling of the news. She'd be a single parent soon, left to raise the girls and manage the family's affairs on her own.

Layla hadn't worked outside of the home since she'd become pregnant with Haily eight years prior. Even then, she had been a low-rate retail manager with income too meager to provide for a family. She had let Trent, an MBA grad, be the breadwinner and handle their finances. Layla's employment prospects didn't look good.

As she stared at the scene in front of her, her husband a shell of the man she once knew who was destined to spend the better part of the rest of his life behind bars, it took every ounce of Layla's mental fortitude to hold herself together without making the kind of dramatic scene she'd been warned about.

Her consciousness was a dense, hot fog of worries and regrets, but a single thought crossed Layla's mind: Her plan had backfired, in a monumental, devastating way.

PART I

THE HOUSEGUEST

1
———

FAMILY TIES

Two Weeks Prior

"Trent, honey," Layla said sweetly through the closed bathroom door. "Breakfast is ready."

She smiled as she listened to the sounds of her husband turning off the shower and grabbing his towel from the bar mounted to the wall nearby.

It was a pretty August morning in Northern California. As usual, a peaceful golden glow was settling over the day. Light streamed in through the large bedroom window where Layla stood.

Before the girls were born, Layla used to sneak into the bathroom for passionate lovemaking sessions as Trent dried off and before he'd had a chance to dress. He'd been so handsome back then, so full of life and vigor. Not that he wasn't attractive to Layla anymore, but now, it felt like they were simply going through the motions.

She thought about unlocking the door with her thumbnail and surprising Trent by stepping inside. The girls were busy in the other room and Layla could surely steal a few passionate minutes with her husband. But she stopped short, assuming he probably wouldn't welcome the intrusion, anyway.

There was a gulf between them that stoked the fires of Layla's rage.

She often felt neglected by her man. With his busy work schedule and the kids, she tended to fall to the bottom of Trent's list of priorities. Layla had tried to remain open and understanding about the distance. After all, she'd been the one who'd asked for the lavish lifestyle they enjoyed. She knew that Trent was the one who'd had to pay the price to get it. And for the time being, he still had a job to go to.

Trent typically worked twelve to fourteen hour days, six days a week. Sometimes seven days a week. But on Saturdays, he never went into the bank until nine or ten in the morning. The family knew they could count on him to stick around long enough for breakfast, and they made the most of it. The girls always made sure to wake up extra early to spend special time with their dad each weekend. Even the family dog, a spotted hound named Romeo, knew to get up and at 'em bright and early on Saturdays.

Layla decided she'd focus on family time. Any special moments between the two of them would have to wait.

"Coming!" Trent replied cheerfully, loud enough for Layla to hear through the door. "Tell Hailey not to eat all the blueberries before I have a chance to put some on top of my pancakes."

Hailey and Trent loved blueberries, while Layla and Bethany preferred strawberries. Since their preferences were evenly divided, they each only had one other person who might eat all of their favorite fruits before they had a chance.

Such matters were trivial given what their family was facing, but it was easier to talk about pancake toppings than what was really going on in their lives. Despite the coolness between husband and wife, Trent's relationship with his girls remained warm.

Layla and Trent hadn't discussed it yet in the light of day, but a few months earlier, their home had been searched by a joint team of investigators from both the Federal Bureau of Investigation and the California Bureau of Investigation. Search warrants had been issued for documents and digital evidence to be collected by forensic experts.

Trent and Layla had been told that information obtained would be analyzed for any evidentiary value. They had nodded obediently as uniformed personnel rifled through their personal items, all while telling the girls it was just a misunderstanding and not to worry. Thanks to the seclusion of the dead end street where the family lived, the incident hadn't turned into a spectacle. Layla was especially grateful for that much.

The Grant family's magnificent home had been custom built a little over a year prior on ten picturesque acres on the outskirts of Rosemary Run.

A white picket fence lined the edge of the property and greeted new arrivals as they entered via the winding driveway. The house was white, too, with black shutters and grand columns that stretched beyond the second story to a majestic gable roofline. Plush landscaping and mature trees framed the home and led to a backyard vegetable garden.

It was drop-dead gorgeous, if Layla did say so herself. She thought it looked every bit as good as the most beautiful local homes featured in Vine Country Magazine.

Rosemary Run was a tourist town, and there was no shortage of breathtaking natural scenery. Beautiful homes with gardens seemed a logical thing to go alongside the region's blessings from Mother Earth.

Layla had been the one to insist on acreage away from the prying eyes of nosy neighbors. It was ironic, really. Layla wanted so badly to impress the people of Rosemary Run, yet she didn't want to associate with them too closely. She wanted to keep them at a safe distance. She *needed* to keep them at a safe distance.

Layla and Trent had secrets from their past that would change the way neighbors saw them, should those secrets be revealed. Layla didn't think about such things on a daily basis, though it remained in the back of her mind. More often than not, her focus was on more mundane daily tasks like taking care of the house, keeping up with the girls and their seemingly endless appointments and commitments, and carving out precious family time whenever she could. The Grants may have been unusual in certain ways, but they were like any other American family in many of the ways that count.

"Looks delicious," Trent remarked as he eagerly joined his wife and daughters at the kitchen table.

A large row of sliding glass doors framed the dining space, stretching behind them and providing an unobstructed view of the pool and fire pit area out back. Layla often thought her daughters took that view for granted. It had been the only one they'd known, after all.

By contrast, Layla appreciated her surroundings. Each and every time she looked out at the stunning scenery, she felt grateful that this was her life. Despite her anger and growing levels of frustration, she maintained perspective on the matter of her comfortable surroundings.

That part was right and good. It wasn't the source of her dissatisfaction.

"I made the pancakes all by myself, Daddy," Hailey chirped, "with the blueberries we picked."

The little girl smiled brightly, longing to soak up every second of her father's attention. She shifted her weight as she talked, forward onto her toes and then back again. One finger absentmindedly twirled a section of long blonde hair.

Both girls were natural blondes, their hair glistening in the sunlight as it streamed through the window. Several beautiful shades were visible in their long, flowing locks. They'd be returning to school for a fresh new year soon, and they'd already planned how they'd style their hair on the first day.

"I helped, too," Bethany added.

"Nuh uh," Hailey replied. "I made the pancakes all by myself. Like I said."

"I helped with the booberries," Bethany said sweetly.

At five, Bethany was old enough to pronounce the word blueberries, but she liked saying boo instead of blue. The innocent term endeared the girl to her big sister, who at age seven was learning to appreciate the differences in people.

Even when agitated, the Grant girls never got too far off kilter. Mild disagreements smoothed out like warm butter when misunderstandings were corrected.

"Oh, yes, you did," Hailey conceded. She turned to her father as she clarified. "Bethany and me picked the blueberries with Mama. They're very delicious."

"I see,' Trent replied. "They look very delicious. But it's Bethany and *I*… not Bethany and *me*…"

Hailey nodded. "Sure, Daddy. Bethany and *I* picked the blueberries with Mama."

"Good girl," Trent said.

Both Hailey and Bethany were bright. They did well in school and aimed to please.

The children positioned themselves on either side of their father as they waited for him to take his first bite. Their grins were broad. Wide enough to cheer up even the most melancholy, in fact. Hailey and Bethany Grant were so happy, so positive, and so upbeat that it was hard for Layla to be depressed around them. Even as she faced a major upheaval in their lives, her girls were a shining bright spot.

"They were good helpers," Layla said, stepping close to the table and tugging gently on Bethany's ponytail as she walked by. "They carried the baskets, even when they got full and heavy."

"What?" Trent joked. "Our girls carried baskets even when their bellies were full. That must have been hard. It's tough to carry baskets on a full belly."

Laughter erupted in the room as the girls reacted. Trent made a bewildered face, amping up the hilarity.

"No, silly," Bethany explained, twirling her hair faster and bouncing on her toes. "*We* weren't full…"

"The *baskets* were full… of blueberries…" Hailey added.

"Ohh," Trent said melodramatically, stretching out his words. "I thought you meant… Hmm…"

"Daddy, you're so silly," Haily said cheerfully.

Romeo woofed from his spot in the corner, getting in on the action as much as a lazy old hound dog could. He wagged his tail slowly, the swish, swish of it sounding softly against the wall.

The girls clapped their hands as Trent finally tasted the blueberry pancakes, his lips curled with pleasure.

"Scrumptious," he said approvingly. "These pancakes are so good, I think I could eat them every morning for the rest of my life."

Hailey nodded, her little chin bobbing up and down.

"Will you make them for me every morning, for the rest of my life?" Trent asked the eldest Grant child, jokingly.

She looked down, bashful. "Not when I'm grown up. I'll have to live in my own house then, Daddy."

Trent raised his brows, then glanced at Layla. Neither wanted to be reminded of how fast the girls were growing up. Or of how soon the four of them might be separated.

"Can't we live in this house together forever? Just like we do now?" he asked.

"Forever!" Bethany agreed. "Mama and Daddy will

take care of us forever, Hailey," she explained to her sister.

Little did the young girl know what troubles awaited. Her parents might not be able to take care of her next month or next year, let alone forever.

"We'll certainly do our best," Layla replied, glancing at her husband before smiling at her girls.

"Mama's right," Trent said, his tone serious. "You know we'd do anything for you girls, don't you? We'll do our very best."

Hailey and Bethany nodded their understanding, but they couldn't possibly know the weight of the words their parents spoke. Layla and Trent *would* do anything for their girls. They both loved their children fiercely and would protect them at all costs.

Unfortunately, though, there were limits. Limits that were imposed by law and order and the precarious circumstances the Grants found themselves in. If only it were a matter of good intentions.

"We know, we know," Hailey said, her tone bored. "You tell us all the time."

"That's because we want you to remember our words," Trent said. "If for some reason we aren't here with you one day in the future, Mama and I want you to remember our words and know that you are very important to us. You are so loved."

"We know, Daddy," Hailey reiterated. "We're loved. You and Mama are too."

Trent wrapped a protective arm around each of his daughters, pulling them close. He leaned his chin down against Hailey's head.

Layla's stomach flopped inside her as she watched the scene, her emotions a mix of positive and negative, happy and sad. She wished she could somehow save her girls from the fate that awaited them.

As the oldest sibling, it would be up to Hailey to help comfort her little sister when things got difficult, as they inevitably would. Hailey would have to grow up fast. Way too fast. Bethany would have to grow up fast, too, but she'd have her big sister to help cushion the harsh realities of the world.

Again, Layla wished she could do something to stop the avalanche of destruction that had taken aim upon her family.

"Let's all eat," she said, redirecting everyone to the task in front of them. "Bethany, honey, will you pass me the strawberries?"

Taking their mother's cue, the girls sat back down in their chairs and went about the business of eating breakfast.

Juice and syrup was poured, butter spread, powdered sugar sprinkled, and fruit piled high on each plate. They ate hungrily. Perhaps they needed to fill themselves to withstand the onslaught to come. Or perhaps Layla and Trent's nervous energy permeated their home, spreading to their girls and making them all wish to soothe themselves any way they could. Either way, they ate and ate.

No one spoke during breakfast. The silence was heavy.

Layla thought she'd break the silence by inviting the

girls to help her in the garden later, when Trent left for work, but the doorbell rang before she had a chance.

"Were you expecting someone?" she asked her husband, her voice full of worry even though she tried to hide it.

The Grant family didn't get many visitors given their secluded location. After the early-morning search conducted by the feds, they were a little jumpy.

Trent shook his head. "No. Are you?"

Layla shook her head in reply. "Shit, shit, shit," she mumbled, barely loud enough for the girls to hear her.

"You said a bad word, Mama," Bethany chided.

Layla and Trent looked at each other. Distress and urgency lined their faces as silent communication spewed from their eyes. They were concerned. They were right to be. The caller at the front door was not a friend. No where close.

"Girls," Layla said in the most authoritative voice she could muster, "go to your rooms. Right now."

"Lock the doors and don't come out," Trent added reluctantly, "until you hear the code word."

"But Daddy…" Hailey began.

"I'm serious, girls," Trent replied. "Go now!"

They scrambled up the stairs, having practiced for just such an event. Hailey and Bethany knew the code word. And they knew what to do while they waited to hear it. They had practiced many, many times.

2

DING DONG

"Coming!" Layla said as she marched toward the front door alongside her husband.

"Don't sound so friendly," he urged. "We don't know what we're dealing with yet."

Layla nodded. Trent was right. Better to be more reserved. Less accommodating. At least, until they found out what this was all about.

The couple had discussed the possibility of unknown and unwanted visitors. They'd been aware that new dangers might present themselves, given the exposure resulting from Trent's criminal case.

The doorbell rang again, longer and more insistently. It sounded like the person pushing it had held it down a few extra seconds for emphasis.

"Okay, okay," Layla said.

She was afraid, but she was also growing angry.

"Who the hell do they think they are?" she asked.

Trent shook his head. "Stay calm, Layla. Don't go flying off the handle and making things worse."

She elbowed her husband. "Don't try to muzzle me."

"What?" he asked incredulously.

The good nature he'd shown just minutes before with the girls was gone now. Out came the darker side of Trent Grant. The one Layla had to reckon with. He was a good man, but he had his moments. And his secrets.

"You always want to silence me. To quiet my frustrations as if they aren't important," she said. "I'm growing weary of this whole song and dance."

The doorbell rang again, followed by three sharp knocks. Whoever was outside was growing impatient.

Trent placed a hand on the door knob, eying his wife before turning it.

"If someone needs to go, let it be me," he said.

"I can handle myself," she replied. "You don't need to be a hero, Trent. For God's sake."

"We've talked about this," he said emphatically as he opened the door. "Me first. It has to be that way. The girls need you."

The door swung open and a stocky man with jet black hair and a handlebar mustache stood outside. He was alone. Despite the unusual mustache, he looked menacing.

"Hello, sir," Trent said, pretending this was something other than what he knew it to be. "How can we help you today?"

The man grunted, and Layla couldn't help but think about how he could easily overpower Trent in a physical fight now that her husband had grown round and soft. This man had big, bulging muscles peeking out from the lines of his fitted shirt.

"You Grant?" the man asked.

Trent nodded as a bead of perspiration formed on his brow. "Yes, sir. Trent and Layla. What can we do for you?"

The man narrowed his eyes, then slowly looked them both up and down. Something about him gave Layla the creeps. She figured Trent felt the same way.

Glancing around, Layla noticed that there was no automobile in sight. Had this man arrived on foot?

"Sir," she tried, "are you lost? Do you need directions? Because the main strip in Rosemary Run is a few miles to the northeast of here. It seems like we're far out, but it's actually…"

The man raised a thick hand in the air to stop her.

"Silence," he snapped.

Layla obeyed. She was committed to playing the role of a typical, nonthreatening housewife. If this man didn't know any better, she certainly wouldn't tell him.

"You," he growled, motioning to Trent. "Outside. We have a business matter to discuss."

Trent pursed his lips. He seemed to be considering his options. Everyone knew he wouldn't refuse. That wasn't part of the deal.

"I can join you, if it isn't too much trouble," Layla tried. "It's a nice morning. Weather's pleasant…"

The man put his beefy hand in the air again, cutting Layla off.

"You," he said, motioning for her to retreat. "Inside the house. Go."

Who did this man think he is, coming to Layla's house and bossing her around like this? He had some nerve. Her blood boiled.

Trent took a deep breath. "It's okay, honey," he said sweetly to his wife, as if they were the picture of domestic bliss. "Go on inside. I'll have a chat with this kind gentleman and I'll be back in a jiffy."

"A jiffy?" Layla asked.

They were supposed to act like a normal, happily married couple, but the term jiffy seemed overboard.

Trent raised his brows, then pointed to the half-way open door behind him. Layla thought about protesting. About insisting that she stay. She had every right to be involved. Why should Trent be elevated to a position above her own? How was that fair? She was every bit as smart and capable as he was. Maybe even more so. But Layla didn't object. She remembered what her husband had said about the girls before he'd opened the door. They'd need her.

"Okay," she said. "I'll be inside-- within earshot-- so, let me know if you boys need anything. Just yell and I'll come right out."

"Thanks, honey," Trent said, then kissed his wife on the cheek as she passed him.

The kiss was an unusual gesture. It gave Layla pause. Something about it struck her as a parting action. Like maybe Trent feared he might not see her again. Like maybe he was thanking her for the good times they'd shared.

She shook her head, hoping to shake free of those morbid thoughts.

"Um hmm," she replied as she stepped inside and closed the door behind her.

Peering through a living room window, Layla watched

the man point to a spot down the driveway. Trent nodded his agreement, then the two set off towards it, their footsteps soft against the pavement.

She thought about calling out to the girls to tell them to stay in their rooms and to stay quiet, but she decided that might draw attention to their presence. If this man was dangerous, Layla would rather he didn't know there were children here. She thought about calling the police, too, but didn't dare. If this man's visit had anything to do with what she believed it might, police involvement was the last thing any of them needed. She'd avoid that at all costs.

She wasn't sure what to do, exactly, other than keep an eye on her husband and wait.

As Layla watched Trent and their visitor make their way up the driveway, Romeo sauntered into the living room and plopped his lazy bones down next to Layla's feet.

"Some guard dog you are," she scoffed. "You didn't even bother to follow the girls upstairs when we sent them up."

The hound raised a brow, then flopped listlessly to one side.

Layla made a mental note to consider a more formidable pet. A German Shephard maybe. Or something that looked big, at least, like a Great Dane. She quickly scratched that idea, though. There wasn't time to raise and train a new animal. The trouble that was coming for the Grants would be here far too soon for that luxury.

While she waited on Trent to return from his business discussion with the mysterious man in the mustache,

Layla went over possible outcomes in her mind. None were pleasant. The likelihood that the strange man's visit was a misunderstanding or something benign seemed slim. It was more probable that the visit spelled trouble. It was hard to say whether that trouble would manifest itself now or later, but surely, it would manifest itself at some point. No good could come of this, Layla was sure of it.

To soothe her nerves, she pulled the mobile phone out of her pocket and dialed her Aunt Tabby, the only living person other than Trent who knew the Grant family's secrets. Most of them, anyway.

"Laylay?" Tabby answered, using the nickname she called her niece when they were in private.

If anyone else had called Layla that, she would have been irritated. Angry at the slight, even. Laylay was a juvenile nickname. For Tabby, though, she'd allow it. That woman had been a Godsend. And Layla knew Tabby had her best interests at heart.

"I'm here," Layla whispered into the phone.

There wasn't a need to be quiet. Not that Layla knew of, anyway. Trent and the man were a good distance from the house now and the girls were in their rooms upstairs. No one else was around.

"Why are we whispering?" Tabby asked, matching Layla's tone.

"A man came to the house and said he needed to speak to Trent alone outside," she explained to her aunt.

"Oh?" Tabby replied. "That's unusual. What do you make of it?"

"I don't know," Layla said, peering out the window

again to see if anything had changed. "The guy gave me the creeps."

"Tell me more."

Layla raised a shoulder and a brow while keeping the phone pressed to one ear. She didn't dare put it on speaker in case the girls might overhear.

"He's odd," she explained. "He has a weird mustache."

"You met him?" Tabby asked.

"Yes, when he first rang the doorbell. Trent and I went out together… after we sent the girls to their rooms."

She didn't need to spell it out. Tabby knew what Layla meant. In fact, Tabby had been given the code word should she ever need to get the girls when both Layla and Trent were unavailable.

Hailey and Bethany didn't know their Great-aunt Tabby possessed the code word. They didn't know Tabby wasn't really their aunt either. She was the closest thing they had, though. The title was honorary.

"I see," Tabby said. "Do you think he's…?"

She didn't need to finish that sentence. Layla knew what Tabby meant.

"I don't know," Layla replied in a hush. "Probably not. Well, then again… maybe."

"Really?"

"Like I said," Layla repeated, "I don't know. Honestly, Tabby, I don't."

"Hmm."

Layla sighed. "This damn hound dog is no help. You'd think he'd be able to sniff out a bad guy. Maybe bark or something."

"He didn't?"

"Ha! He didn't so much as get up from his spot in the corner of the dining room until I'd been outside and come back in," Layla said. "Then he just meandered in and went back to dozing. No sense of concern about Trent being out there with the mystery man."

Tabby was quiet for a moment, thinking. Meanwhile, Layla began to pace back and forth in front of the window.

"It sounds like I should come over," Tabby said. "Pay everyone a little visit. Maybe that will encourage this guy to buzz off."

"What if he recognizes you?" Layla asked before she thought better of it.

Tabby went silent again, and Layla wished she hadn't said what she did. She knew she should be more careful. Especially over the phone. Anyone could be listening on the line.

"Sorry, Tab," she breathed.

"It's okay," Tabby replied. "But I'm coming over. We'll take it from there. Watch for me?"

"Of course," Layla confirmed. "I'll keep my eyes peeled. I'll come out when you arrive, whether Trent's done with the man or not."

"Good. Give me fifteen. On my way."

Layla smiled as she hung up the phone. Tabby would know what to do. She was sure of it.

LITTLE VOICES

"Mommy?" a little voice called from an upstairs bedroom. "Please come here. I'm scared."

It was Bethany. Layla would know her voice anywhere. The girl was supposed to be silent, though. They had practiced for this.

Layla wasn't sure whether today was a false alarm. Even if so, she suspected the real thing would happen one day soon. Trent's criminal situation was drawing unwanted attention to the family.

The Grants had lived a peaceful life under the radar for a long while. So long, in fact, that Layla and Trent had become accustomed to normal, small-town American life. But now that Trent was in trouble with the law, their quiet existence was bound to end. It was just a matter of when and how dramatically things would unravel.

"Shh," she whispered up the stairs.

It probably wasn't loud enough for Bethany to hear. Layla debated whether to go and comfort the child. She knew this must be scary for the girls. It was scary for her, too, but it was important that they all be prepared.

"Stay quiet and still until you hear the code word," Layla said, louder this time.

She listened for a response but only heard muffled crying.

"Oh, Bethany," she mouthed. "You're breaking my heart, my little dear."

Layla leaned on the banister at the bottom of the stairs as she worked to maintain control of her emotions. Maintaining control was important, for sure, but it wasn't always easy.

Bethany was only five-years-old. Far too young to understand the intricacies of her parents' situation. Even at seven, Hailey couldn't understand them either.

What was Layla to do? She wondered how to protect children who were far too young to protect themselves.

Here she had successfully made a normal life for the four of them in Rosemary Run. She and Trent both had. Maybe doing so had been a mistake. Only, they'd had no choice. Not really. Welcoming children into the world and becoming a family had been an important part of staying under the radar. They'd all seemed less suspicious that way. Trent and Layla blended in more. People took less notice of them, other than to note what a nice, normal family they were.

But in Layla's world, success was a moving target. Right now, it meant surviving the coming weeks and months, and making sure her girls were safe. First and foremost, they needed to be kept *physically* safe. As for emotional safety, well, that was a taller order. Layla vowed to do what she could.

Suddenly, she heard a loud engine moving swiftly out front.

"Tabby?" she asked out loud.

Layla moved back to the window, pulling the curtain away and looking out. To her dismay, it wasn't Tabby. Not yet, anyway. She'd known that when she'd first heard the engine, but she hadn't wanted it to be true. Trent was out there exposed and vulnerable.

"Who's there?" she asked quietly.

Asking the questions out loud was comforting, for some reason. It made Layla feel less alone, even though no one was in the house with her except for the girls hiding upstairs in their rooms.

Romeo groaned, as if Layla was disturbing him. He shifted his weight, flopping over to his other side in the process, his long ears dragging against the hardwood.

"Please, dog," she said, "not now."

Outside, a disturbing scene was unfolding. A black, military-style vehicle with angular lines and few windows was now parked in the Grants' driveway near Trent and the strange man with the mustache. It wasn't the kind of vehicle you'd expect to see in Rosemary Run, that was for sure. It wasn't the kind of vehicle that could blend in without the risk of drawing unwanted attention, either.

Whatever this thing was, it couldn't be good.

Layla watched as two doors on either side of the vehicle opened from the bottom, raising into the air like wings. The man with the mustache didn't so much as glance at it, which meant that he was already familiar. Also not good.

She saw Trent's body language change ever so slightly. His shoulders tensed, and he tilted his head forward, chin down and eyes up. Layla knew her husband well enough to realize that he was nervous. He had the look of a man who was aware that he might just meet his maker. That his fate wasn't in his own hands. Not anymore.

Instinctively, Layla moved to the door and grabbed the handle. She wanted to go to him. They were in this together, after all. They had been since the start. This was their family, and Layla intended to do everything in her power to protect it. That meant protecting Trent, too. Only, she wasn't sure how she'd do so.

There were weapons stashed in the basement. Big ones. But breaking those out would escalate the situation. Not to mention, it would take a few minutes to go down and get them. In those few minutes, someone could enter the house and get closer to the girls. Layla certainly couldn't let that happen. She decided it was best-- for now-- to stick around and keep an eye on the front entrance. And to keep up appearances of being a typical, nonthreatening housewife.

But she couldn't leave Trent to face this danger on his own. Ignoring his plea to stay inside and to let him handle this, Layla burst out the front door, mobile phone in hand.

"Trent!" she called. "Aunt Tabby is on the way. I just spoke to her on the phone."

She didn't know what else to say. She was winging it at this point. Hoping these odd visitors would decide to leave her family alone.

"Go back inside," Trent said solemnly. "We're okay out here."

He didn't sound okay. Layla stared at him hard, pleading with her eyes, though Trent was likely too far away to see his wife's features clearly.

"Tabby said she has important news to share," she tried. "Something she insisted she tell us in person. Should I pour you a glass of lemonade for our chat?"

Layla considered inviting the visitors in for lemonade, too, as a courtesy, but thought better of it. Those uninvited guests needed to go away, and fast.

The man with the mustache raised his thick hand to silence Layla once more. It was quick, and he didn't bother to look at her when he did it. The move struck her as pompous, and it stoked the fires of the rage that burned constantly in the background of her emotions. Anger flared inside her.

Trent noticed. He didn't have to see the fine details of his wife's features to know his wife was about to blow her top. And he knew what might happen if Layla became angry. He didn't want things to take that turn. He was trying hard to lower tensions, not intensify them. Their lives depended on it.

"Honey," he tried, careful not to use his wife's name, just in case anonymity provided any additional measure of protection. "We'll talk about Tabby when I'm finished here. I'm having a private discussion. It doesn't concern you. I promise we'll catch up later."

Trent looked hard at his wife, hoping desperately to keep her from making a scene. He feared what might happen if she challenged these people. But from such a distance, she couldn't see the concern in his face. She wouldn't have paid attention, anyway.

Layla was tired of being dismissed-- on a life scale. Tired of being seen as just a housewife and a mother without talents or skills of her own. That wasn't the way it was supposed to be. It wasn't what she'd signed up for.

Stiffening, she started down the stairs, her feet landing hard with each step. The warm morning air wrapped itself around her. She wanted to go to Trent and have a stern talk with the mustached man and his associates in the angular car.

How dare that man treat her so poorly? He didn't know her. He didn't know anything about her. At least, not enough to treat her like a second-class citizen. Nobody got to do that.

"Honey, go inside!" Trent implored. "Come now. You must listen to what I'm telling you. I'm okay out here. *We're* okay out here. Leave us be."

Layla shook her head as she planned her next move. Pulling from her best acting chops, she turned on her syrupy sweet, concerned wife persona.

"I'd like to join you, if that's alright," she said as she turned toward the driveway and began her ascent uphill. "I could bring some lemonade out here. We could share some with our guests-- including Tabby, when she gets here."

Layla ignored the mustached man and his hand signals as she forged on, determined to defend herself and offer some kind of assistance to Trent. Until a small voice stopped her. The weight of the world was contained in that gentle voice.

She heard it from the window upstairs. It was Bethany again. The young girl had cracked her bedroom window and was calling to her mom through the open space.

"Mommy! Come back! Please!" Bethany called.

The request stopped Layla in her tracks.

She stiffened again, this time out of terrible fear. She wasn't sure if the mustached man had heard the girl or not. The motor was still running on the strange vehicle and the man's back was to the house now, so maybe not. No one had emerged from the vehicle yet.

Layla glanced at Trent, who tipped his head enough to signal his awareness of their daughter in the window. Their girls were their priority. On that, they agreed wholeheartedly. Biting back her anger, Layla turned for the safety of the house.

"If you say so, honey," she called to Trent. "I'll be waiting inside."

He nodded, relieved. So relieved that his shoulders visibly relaxed and his posture improved. Trent cared about his family. That much was obvious.

"Watch for Tabby, though," Layla added, hoping it might delay whatever was about to happen. "She'll be around soon. And she insists we have a lot to talk about."

"Will do," Trent replied.

His tone was cautious, his words measured. Layla didn't like the sound of it. She wished she had more control over the situation. She wanted to do more. To *be* more in this moment. She hated feeling like her hands were tied.

As she climbed the steps on her way back to the front entrance, she noticed the door was slightly ajar. She thought she had closed the door behind her. In fact, she was sure of it.

Layla leaned forward, hesitantly. She didn't hear anything else from inside the house, though the rush of her pounding pulse swished in her ears. Bethany had gone quiet again, probably appeased by seeing her mother turn back. All was silent upstairs. The motor still hummed in the driveway but it was the only sound that could be heard out front, other than the muffled voices of Trent and the odd man.

Suddenly, Romeo ran out of the house, nosing his way through the cracked door so that it opened up wide enough for his pudgy body. His ears were back and he moved faster than Layla had ever seen him go. Not since he was a young pup, anyway. His demeanor wasn't right. It alarmed her.

"Romeo! Get back here!" she shouted as she chased the dog around the side of the house.

He didn't have a leash attached and wasn't otherwise restrained, which gave him the run of the property. By the looks of him, he intended to make full use of it.

"Romeo!" Layla tried again, though he paid little attention. "Come on, boy. Seriously!"

The dog was scared of something. This wasn't just a joyful jaunt in the morning sun. He'd been spooked and was running with that in mind. He moved in the way only a scared animal can, all adrenaline and survival instinct.

The girls would be devastated if something happened to their pup. And historically, Romeo wasn't great around cars or roads. He didn't seem to have a sense about them. Layla had meant to do something about that issue-- to have Romeo trained better or to install an invisible fence around the edge of the property-- but she hadn't gotten around to it. Now she wished she had.

"Romeo! I mean it," she implored. "Come back here, right now!"

She saw him bounding across the side yard and dangerously close to where the road curved near the neighboring lot. Before she could catch up with him, she heard another vehicle approaching. It was Tabby's pickup truck this time. Layla recognized the sputtering of its aging muffler and turned to see her friend turning into the driveway.

"Tabby!" she called, waving, making sure to put on a good show for the odd man and his colleagues in the angular vehicle.

Everything Layla did felt like a knee-jerk reaction. She wasn't controlling her emotions. She knew that much for sure.

She'd been taught to remain focused and restrained at all times. That was before she'd had a husband and children. Things felt different now. She wasn't even sure she wanted her old life. Only, another part of her wanted it more than anything. The jumble of emotions left a cool, metallic taste in her mouth.

Tabby honked her horn in three short, friendly beeps as the truck came to a stop behind the other vehicle. Seemingly fearless, the woman cut the ignition and stepped out, walking right over to Trent and the mustached man as if they'd been expecting her.

"Howdy," Tabby said.

Her voice was so loud that Layla could hear it from a distance.

Tabby hailed from the Texas hills, and she had the accent to prove it. Her short, silver, curly hair fit neatly into a cowboy hat. She often wore one, hoop earrings swinging below as red lipstick lined her mouth. Layla noticed that she wasn't wearing a hat today, though. Maybe she'd left it in the truck.

"Hey, there," Trent replied. "How's it going?"

Layla scoffed, instantly irritated by her husband's choice of words. Her feelings about him could turn on a dime, and they often did.

"Going good," Tabby replied. "Who's your friend?"

4

FRIENDS AND COUNTRYMEN

As if on cue, Romeo darted toward the gathering in the driveway. His floppy ears trailed behind him as he hurled his body awkwardly past the mustached man and plopped down on Trent's feet.

"Grab him!" Layla called as she made her way down the driveway to join the others. "I'm afraid he'll get into the road and get himself run over."

She almost said something about how the girls would be devastated, but she stopped herself. This man didn't need to know there were children here, if they didn't already.

"I've got him," Trent said as he bent down and scooped the dog into his arms.

"Ornery little guy, isn't he?" Tabby asked, ignoring the strange man and the unusual vehicle.

Trent sighed. "Yeah, he's a good boy, but he isn't the smartest dog we've ever known."

"You can say that again," Layla added, arriving at her husband's side.

She wasn't positive, but she thought she saw the mustached man's brow twitch when he heard her voice. He didn't bother to make eye contact.

This guy, Layla thought. *I ought to…*

"Will you take Romeo inside?" Trent asked Layla in a serious tone, eyeing his wife.

Tabby pretended to look confused. She crossed her long arms over her chest, the wrinkles around her elbows made more prominent by the pose. Tabby was a beautiful woman, no doubt about it, but she wasn't a young, fit woman any longer. Years of sitting while driving the school bus had made her soft. If things went bad out here, she wouldn't be able to run fast enough to get away.

Neither would Trent, for that matter.

"Aren't you going to introduce us first?" Tabby asked, glancing back and forth from Trent to the mustached man.

Trent took in a sharp breath, his eyes pleading with Tabby to let it go. She would do no such thing, and he knew it. Like Layla, Tabby wanted to help Trent. She considered him family. She wasn't sure what she could do to help but she intended to try. She wouldn't go down without a fight.

"I'm Ivan," the man said in a deep, gruff voice.

His gaze remained fixed on the road in the distance. He didn't seem the least bit concerned about manners or pleasantries. Although, offering his name was more than Layla had expected. Assuming Ivan was his real name.

"Ivan who?" Tabby asked.

He dropped his brows so low that it seemed like they might swallow his eyes. Apparently, Ivan wasn't a big fan of assertive women. Maybe he wasn't a fan of women, in general. Either way, his reaction irritated Layla.

He paused for a moment, considering. "Ivan Semenov," he replied. "Why do you ask?"

"Is that your real name?" Tabby probed.

"Yes, it is." He put his hands on his hips, his body growing tense.

Tabby was relentless. She was, apparently, determined to put this man on notice. She wanted him to know that they wouldn't take trouble lying down. Layla appreciated her friend's spirit. She was worried, though. Worried that they were playing with fire. Fire that might very well burn her precious little girls.

"You Russian?" Tabby persisted.

Ivan's brows went even lower. He pursed his lips as his nostrils flared. "Yes. I am a proud Russian. What are you?"

Tabby smirked. "Like a bad guy in an action movie," she mused, turning to Trent and Layla. "Ivan the Russian. Would you believe this if you weren't seeing it live and in person?"

Trent shook his head, not to agree with Tabby but to insist that she stop. She would make a huge mess of things if she wasn't careful, and Trent knew it. He widened his eyes and cleared his throat, unsure of what to say. "Don't be rude to our guest," he managed.

Layla remained perfectly still except for one hand that scratched Romeo's silky head absentmindedly as Trent cradled the dog in his arms. She was angry, but knew better than to let the others know it.

It would be different if it weren't for the girls. If Layla weren't a mother.

Ivan took a step toward Tabby, bringing his boot down hard against the ground in front of her. "I asked you a question, woman. Answer me."

Tabby turned her head slowly, making a show out of her defiance. Her brown skin glistened in the morning light as her cheeks lifted into a smile. She wasn't afraid of Ivan, and he knew it.

"Forgive my friend," Layla interrupted. "She's crabby in the morning before she's had her coffee. Right, Tabby?"

Trent shot Layla a look that said to be careful. It was so very important that she stand down. That she remain respectful of Ivan's power over the Grant family. Like it or not, they were at his mercy.

Ivan grunted and spit on the ground in front of him, his saliva landing just inches from Tabby's feet.

"Oh, no," Layla whispered, loud enough for Trent to hear.

Tabby gritted her teeth and stood up even straighter. "I'm a proud American, Ivan Semenov. The name's Tabatha Rhodes. I come from the great state of Texas. We don't like outsiders much."

"Good thing we aren't in your state of Texas," Ivan said with a sinister laugh. "Look around and see where we are."

He waved one thick hand around him for emphasis.

For the first time, Layla heard voices inside the angular vehicle. She could make out at least three distinct laughs responding to Ivan's remarks.

This wasn't good. If these guys really were Russian,

the Grant family was in grave danger. Layla knew that for sure. There was a history to be considered. One that promised dreadful certainties.

Tabby was a comfort to Layla and Trent given the way she wanted to protect her friends, but she'd be in danger, too. Especially due to her cavalier attitude toward Ivan.

Layla knew she had to do something to end this. Even if it meant that Trent had to deal with these guys by himself, then so be it. Maybe he'd been right when he'd told Layla to stay inside and think of the girls. Keeping them safe was most important. It broke Layla's heart to think of leaving Trent out here alone, but she knew what she had to do.

"Tabby, I was just about to make some fresh lemonade. Why don't we go inside and pour ourselves a glass?" Layla asked, pushing her anger down and hoping her friend could find a way to do the same.

Tabby sighed heavily, hands on her hips in a pose that mimicked Ivan's.

"Yes, women inside," Ivan grunted. "The men will go for a little ride."

Trent gasped, unable to hide his reaction upon learning that Ivan intended to take him somewhere.

They all knew better than to let someone threatening take them to a secondary location. It was common sense, really. Once bad guys have you in their grips, they can do with you what they wish. It rarely ends well from there. Everyone knows that.

Trent's complexion flushed, turning from its usual pale pink to a hot, throbbing red.

Layla again thought about calling the police. She and

Tabby made eye contact, and they were both thinking the same thing. But Layla knew that wasn't wise. Not given her family's particular history and vulnerabilities. No, it was better to leave police out of this if at all possible. Especially since Trent was in white-collar trouble. Anything additional would complicate matters beyond good reason.

"Women inside?" Tabby asked. "What kind of b.s. are you spewing?"

She seemed to be deciding how far to push this.

"That lemonade?" Layla prompted, placing a firm hand on Tabby's shoulder.

In the distance, Layla thought she heard Bethany call out her name again. Trent must have heard it, too, because he sprang into action, handing the dog to his wife and playing the part of an unsuspecting, cooperative husband.

"Layla's lemonade is delicious," Trent said to Tabby. "It's fresh squeezed with lemons from a tree in our backyard. If you haven't tasted it yet, you should. And if you have, well, then you know that you don't want to miss a chance to taste it again. Besides, I'm happy to take a ride with Ivan. No worries."

The perspiration on Trent's brow told another story, but he didn't have much choice when it came right down to it. He'd do anything to protect his family.

Layla hoisted Romeo onto one hip, then took hold of her friend's hand. "Come, Tabby," she pleaded. "Let's go inside."

Tabby resisted at first, eyeing Ivan and thinking the

situation through. Finally, though, she acquiesced and allowed Layla to lead her toward the front of the house.

"Another time, Ivan Semenov," Tabby muttered as she walked away. "I suspect we'll meet again."

"It will be my pleasure, American woman," Ivan replied sarcastically.

Tabby grunted in response. "Don't scrape my truck when you back that monstrosity out of the driveway," she quipped.

Luckily, Ivan her slight go without responding aggressively. He didn't need to respond yet. He had the real power in the situation, and soon enough, Tabby and the Grants would learn exactly how much control over their lives he truly had.

The woman turned and walked quickly toward the front of the Grants' home, the shuffling of their feet the only sound in what suddenly felt like an eerily quiet scene. Even Romeo remained silent as he bobbed along on Layla's hip, his ears flopping in the gentle breeze. It seemed like the dog had worn himself out and was ready to plop back down for a nap just as soon as they got back inside.

Layla silently willed Bethany to stay quiet. If the girl called out for her mother now, Ivan would certainly hear her.

"Where to?" Trent asked in his best unassuming voice.

Layla closed her eyes when she heard her husband speak, conflicted by the desire to help him and the strong urge to keep their girls from harm.

"He'll be okay," Tabby breathed. "If you ask me, that Russian is all bark and no bite."

"I disagree," Layla replied. She knew the threat was real.

"He's got you all hyped up for nothing," Tabby added, her demeanor confident and sure.

Suddenly, Layla froze in her tracks, her eyes fixed on the front door.

"What is it?" Tabby asked. "Did you leave the door open? Is that how the dog got out?"

Layla shook her head slowly, her mind processing the details of the danger her eyes were seeing. Without responding to Tabby, she rushed forward, pushing her way through the open door and into the house.

"Wait!" Tabby called, hustling to catch up. "What's happening right now?"

Layla slammed the door behind her, letting it close in Tabby's face. Her worst fears had risen to the surface. She wasn't the least bit concerned about Tabby at that moment. She set Romeo down, dropping him from knee height instead of taking the time to lower him to the floor. There wasn't time.

Layla wanted to call out to the girls but she knew that whomever was in the house would hear her. If they weren't already aware of the girls' presence, she wouldn't tip them off.

She moved from room to room, scanning her surroundings and searching for clues as to who had entered her family's safe space. The hairs on the back of her neck stood on end.

Someone was there. She could feel it.

5

———

NO SAFE SPACE

"Mama!" Bethany called.

Her voice was an unnatural timbre. Layla could immediately tell that her baby girl was terrified. So terrified, in fact, that the plan and the code word had been discarded.

Damn, damn, damn, Layla thought.

"Go back!" Layla shrieked, more fear in her voice than in her daughter's. "Get in your room and lock the door. Now!"

Romeo bolted by Layla's feet as he made a nervous run of the house. This wasn't like him at all. The dog's frantic energy heightened Layla's fears even further. Animals knew when something was wrong.

Layla quickly realized that must have been why Romeo had escaped from the house and run wild around the property. Layla hadn't left the door ajar. Someone had entered the house, leaving the door open behind them. She kicked herself for spending time toying with Tabby and Ivan when someone was in her home. Near her little girls.

"I can't," Bethany cried. "I'm too scared, Mama."

Layla's heart grew heavy in her chest, suddenly feeling like it was both sinking and rising into her throat at the same time. She had to get Bethany to safety. And she didn't even know where the intruder was located within the house. It seemed like an impossible task to handle both problems at once.

She needed Tabby. If Tabby would help.

Opening the front door, Layla was relieved to find her friend waiting patiently outside. "I need you," she whispered as she pulled Tabby in by an elbow.

"You're acting strange, Laylay. What's up?"

"Someone is in the house," she replied.

"A bad guy?" Tabby asked.

"Or girl," Layla said. "I don't know. But Bethany is out of her room, crying for me. I need to go to her."

Tabby nodded. "Go. I'll look for the louse."

"The louse?" Layla asked.

Tabby sometimes sounded very old fashioned. Layla often laughed about it. But she didn't have time to do so now. Her girls were in danger.

"Yeah, yeah," Tabby said, anticipating her friend's comment before Layla even had a chance to say it. "Get going."

Layla nodded and started up the stairs. She thought about telling Tabby that guns were in the basement but she didn't want the intruder to find them. She kept that bit of information to herself as she climbed to the second floor, her hands gripping the railings tightly as she rounded the turn to face the exposed landing.

When she arrived at the top of the stairs, it was eerily quiet. Bethany's bedroom door was closed. Not a peep could be heard. Hailey's door was closed, too, which made sense. At two and a half years older, Hailey could be counted on to follow instructions and keep herself hidden. Hopefully, the oldest Grant child was still barricaded and safe.

Layla wanted to call Bethany's name. Only she didn't want to disclose the child's name to the intruder. She also didn't want to confuse matters for Hailey, who would be waiting on the code word. Layla chose her words carefully.

"Honey, I heard you calling for me a few minutes ago. Where are you now?"

There was no reply, which was strange given how upset Bethany sounded. The heaviness in Layla's chest grew more burdensome. She knew with every fiber of her being that something was wrong. Very wrong. Her body trembled as she tried to steady herself, her shoes sticking on the hardwood floor.

"Where are you?" Layla tried again as she made her way to the closed door of Bethany's room and placed her fingers on the round knob.

The wooden, cursive letter B painted pastel pink and hung on the outside of the little girl's door swayed slightly on its hook. Layla knew she hadn't made the fixture move. She'd stepped softly, and she hadn't applied any pressure to the door knob. That meant someone was walking around inside the room.

Layla said a silent prayer that Bethany was alone in there. She pleaded with whatever higher power might hear her and protect her innocent child.

"I'm coming in," she said, tightening her grip on the knob and attempting to turn it. "I'm here, honey."

The door was locked tight. The knob would not turn.

"Mama!" Bethany cried, her little voice muffled this time. "Help, Mama! Help me. Help me. Please!"

Layla's blood ran cold when she heard a deep male voice reply. "Shut up, you rotten brat."

Suddenly, the room began to spin and Layla saw spots. Her world was coming undone in front of her. She'd thought Trent's legal troubles were the worst thing that could have happened to the Grant family. Now she wondered how she could have been so foolish and short sighted. The girls' safety was everything to Layla.

This can't be happening, she thought.

She tugged on the door knob once more, wiggling it back and forth and pulling with all her might. It didn't budge.

She wanted to burst through the door and get to her daughter, yet she knew she probably wasn't strong enough for that. The Grant family home had tall, solid oak interior doors that wouldn't easily move. Trent *might* be able to knock one down, but he was outside and out of ear shot. Besides, Ivan wasn't likely to let the object of his attention leave. He had Trent right where he wanted him.

The man in Bethany's room must be working with Ivan. This must have been planned. And Layla had fallen right into their trap.

"Tabby! Come quickly!" Layla tried. "Beth-- I mean, um-- the girl…"

Layla knew she shouldn't use Bethany's name. She wasn't sure how to communicate without doing so, though. Tabby understood.

"Coming!" Tabby called, her determined footsteps making their way toward Layla.

We're in big trouble, Layla thought. *Big enough trouble to need police involvement. There's no avoiding it now.*

No matter what happened to her or Trent as a result, Layla would do everything possible to keep her children safe. That was the blessing and the curse of being a parent.

She pulled her mobile phone out of her pocket and dialed 9-1-1. Thankfully, the dispatcher picked up right away.

"9-1-1, Officer Devonte Rucker here. What is your emergency?" a smooth baritone voice asked.

"Someone has my daughter!" Layla shouted. "He's in her room! I heard a man's voice. She's crying…"

"Ma'am, stay calm. What is your address?"

"1522 Spice Ridge Road in Rosemary Run," she managed to reply. "Hurry!"

Layla was surprised she could remember her address at a time like this. The room continued to spin around her.

"Stand by, ma'am. Officers are on their way. I'll need you to stay on the line with me until they get there, okay?"

"Okay," Layla mumbled. "Please, tell them to hurry. She's little… five-years-old…"

She wanted to cry, but couldn't. Tears wouldn't come.

She dropped the phone to her side as Tabby reached her, eyes wild with concern.

"I'm here," Tabby said. "Did you call 9-1-1?"

Tabby glanced at the phone in Layla's outstretched hand.

Before Layla could explain anything, Bethany cried out again, her voice still muffled as if something was covering her mouth.

"Mama! Mama!" Bethany pleaded. "He got me!"

"Oh, honey, help is on the way!" Layla said through tears. "Hold on."

Tabby stepped in front of her friend, positioning herself between Layla and Bethany's closed bedroom door. She gently took the phone out of Layla's hand, then ended the call, disconnecting Officer Rucker. She pushed the button to turn the device off, then placed the phone in her own pants pocket. All the while, Tabby maintained eye contact with Layla, her demeanor strangely calm given what was happening.

"What are you doing?" Layla asked. "He told me to stay on the line."

Layla's voice quivered, everything unsteady. She was glad Tabby was there to help steady her. But Tabby was acting strange.

"Trust me," Tabby said.

Layla grimaced. "Why? What are you talking about?"

Tabby took Layla by the shoulders and moved her away from Bethany's door.

"Come with me," Tabby instructed. "I need you to do exactly as I say, if you want your family to make it out of this alive."

Fear flashed through Layla's eyes. She couldn't fathom how things had turned so serious so fast. Less than thirty minutes ago, the family was sitting down to a nice Sunday breakfast. Now Tabby was talking about them not making it out alive.

"Tabby, what the hell?" Layla asked, her body going almost entirely numb from the shock. "I want you to tell me what is going on."

Tabby didn't answer her friend. She simply guided Layla to the master bedroom, led her into a closet, and motioned for her to be quiet.

Layla opened her mouth to protest some more, but Tabby placed a single finger on her friend's lips. They stared at each other for a silent moment, an intense sense of urgency alive between them. Everything was at stake.

Layla wanted to rage against the unfairness of it all. She wanted to scoop her girls up and protect them like a mama bear would, roaring and gnashing teeth if anyone came too close. But she couldn't. The three of them were in separate rooms while Trent was out front, and these men were incredibly dangerous. Layla wasn't equipped to sort this out. She wished she was.

Tabby put a hand on Layla's forearm and gave it a squeeze that said to wait. Tabby understood that this situation had quickly evolved into more than Layla and Trent could handle on their own. The trouble was big. Far bigger than anything prosecutors or a judge could dish out for Trent's white-collar crimes.

Layla wondered how Tabby could possibly know what to do. As far as Layla was aware, her friend was just a retired small-town school bus driver. Could there have been more to Tabby's past? There was more to Layla's past than that of a housewife and mother, which made her think that perhaps Tabby had more to offer than what it might have seemed on the surface.

Layla decided to trust Tabby. After all, what more did she have to lose? As far as she could tell, she was running out of viable options.

"Okay," Layla mouthed. "Do you remember the code word? For the girls?"

Tabby nodded, and Layla said a silent prayer of thanks that she and Trent had shared the code word with their friend. Neither of them had extended family in the area, and Tabby had become the closest thing to family they had. Layla was grateful.

Quickly and quietly, Tabby exited the bedroom closet, leaving Layla alone with her thoughts. Layla heard her friend close and lock the master bedroom door. Now she was locked in like Hailey. She prayed that Tabby would find a way to save them all.

CHILDHOODS

As Layla waited nervously for the ordeal to be over, she reminisced about her life and how it had come to this. She couldn't hear anything from inside the closet, anyway. She was reliant on Tabby to return and bring good news.

Usually, Layla didn't spend time thinking about her childhood and the family she'd left behind. She'd found through years of practice that it was best to look forward rather than to get bogged down in people and things from her past. Trent had felt the same way about the childhood and the family he'd left behind. The couple's shared experiences had bonded them.

If she closed her eyes, Layla could still see the people she'd grown up with. Her mother's kind green eyes, her father's gentle smile, and the shadows of her siblings as they played ball together in the yard next to their humble cottage were still vivid in her memory, all these years later. Her family had been good to her. Her upbringing had included a few emotional bumps and bruises but nothing too terrible.

Something inside Layla had yearned for more. Maybe-- at the heart of it all-- she'd wanted to stand out. She'd always believed that no one with multiple siblings gets noticed unless they work for it.

When she'd first left for a new job and adventure as a young woman, Layla had told herself she'd find a way to get back to her parents someday. Superiors who had walked her path had warned her that returning to her old life wouldn't be possible. She had hoped they were wrong, though. She didn't want them to be right. But she'd pushed the problem away to solve another day.

As months became years and years became decades, that day had never come. Now here she was in a closet, wishing her mom and dad could somehow kiss away the pain and make everything alright like they had when she was a little girl.

It's such a sad story, really, Layla thought.

Trent was the only soul on this Earth who knew the real story about Layla's childhood and the family she'd come from. Not even the girls knew the truth. They'd been told that Layla's parents were killed in a boating accident when she was a teenager. Layla had told Bethany and Hailey she'd had no siblings.

It had been painful to lie, at first. But she'd become used to it. Something about the fact that the Grant girls could be facing an end to their short lives made Layla's heart ache for the extended family who'd never had a chance to know them. Her heart ached for the girls, too, the sweet babes robbed of the opportunity to know grandparents, aunts, uncles, and cousins.

Layla began to wish she'd made different choices in life.

Her decisions had seemed so certain when she'd been younger. So sure. She'd thought she was on a path that would lead her to glory. One that would eventually see her appreciated for her noble efforts in a tough career that not everyone was cut out for. More and more, though, she wondered if she was cut out for it herself. Having the girls had been part of the plan, but Layla hadn't anticipated just how drastically being a mother would change her.

Suddenly, she heard a soft knock at the bedroom door. It was so soft that Layla almost thought she was imagining the sound.

"Mama?" a tender voice called.

It was Hailey. She sounded calm and collected. Mostly. *But how? Why did she come out of her room?*

Layla didn't waste time answering those questions in her own mind. Her daughter was out there, and she intended to get her to safety.

"In here!" she called back. "Come in."

But Hailey didn't come in. Maybe she couldn't get in through the locked door.

Layla leaped from her spot on the closet floor, grabbing a clothes bar to steady herself as she found footing and opened the closet door. She scrambled from the closet across the bedroom, her body moving as swiftly as it could while maneuvering around the king sized bed in the middle of the room.

When she reached the heavy oak door that separated her from Hailey, Layla unlocked the knob and flung the door wide open without considering what might await her on the other side.

Although, a mama bear doesn't care what's on the other side. Layla would probably have opened the door anyway.

"Oh, no," Layla gasped when she saw, one hand flying to cover her open mouth.

There, standing in front of her, was Hailey. But she wasn't alone. A big, brooding man stood with her. He was dressed in all black and had a shaved head, dark stubble framing his jaw. He looked a lot like Ivan, as if they'd been cut from the same cloth. In his beefy arms, he held Bethany. The youngest Grant girl had been knocked out. Or maybe she was sleeping. Layla couldn't tell. She wasn't sure it mattered. This man had his hands on her child.

Layla's limbs instantly went numb at the sight of both her girls under this man's control.

"The code word," Layla mumbled. "How,,,?"

"I'm sorry, Mama," Hailey replied. "He told me he'd hurt Bethany if I didn't do what he said. I didn't want her to get hurt."

Layla's eyes rolled back into her head as she fought to stay conscious. Her mouth was suddenly dry, as if it had been stuffed full of cotton. She grew lightheaded, ready to faint.

She couldn't bring herself to address the man holding her girls. Not yet.

"Where's Aunt Tabby?" she asked her daughter.

"I don't know," Hailey replied. "I haven't seen her."

"Not at all?" Layla asked, surprised.

The words stuck on her tongue. It took a tremendous amount of effort to get them out.

Layla had thought Tabby would get the girls to safety. What had happened while she'd been hiding in the closet? She wasn't sure how long she'd been in there. Time had seemed to move and bend along with her terror. Her pleasant childhood memories had been the only comfort.

"No, not today," Hailey confirmed. "Why? Was she here?"

The big man chuckled. It seemed like he was enjoying this.

"What are you laughing at?" Layla sputtered, raising her eyes to meet his.

"Nothing," he replied.

He kept a smile on his lips, which Layla thought was pompous, given the circumstances. His voice was rough as sandpaper. It grated on her ears.

"What do you want with us?" she asked. "You should let my girls go. They're innocent children. They haven't done anything to you."

"I'm not calling the shots," the man said. "I have a boss, and he wants you held. All three of you."

Layla lowered her brow as Hailey leaned against her. At least, this guy was letting mother and daughter embrace. It was a small comfort, but one that didn't go unnoticed.

"Held for what?" Layla continued.

The man laughed again, more heartily this time. "You don't know?"

Layla shook her head.

"You're his insurance policy," he explained. "I stay with you so your husband will cooperate."

Hailey's eyes grew wide. Apparently, she hadn't realized her father was in danger. "Where's Daddy?" she asked, her voice quivering.

Her daughter's distress hit Layla like a spear through the heart. She'd always worried that the girls could someday fall into harm's way as a result of their parents' choices, but seeing it happen was crushing. How unfair life was. Layla again kicked herself for allowing this to come to pass. She blamed herself. Although, Trent certainly had responsibility, too.

Looking at the man, Layla knew it would be best if she explained. She knew more than she wanted to about who these people were and why they were here. Hailey would be able to take it better coming from her.

"He went for a ride with someone from work," Layla said. "I expect he'll be back soon."

The big man nodded his approval. Apparently, he didn't intend to hurt the girls. Not right now, anyway.

Hailey seemed confused. "Is this man from Daddy's work?"

Layla nodded.

"At the bank?"

She nodded again. "I know it seems scary, but everything is going to be okay."

Hailey chewed her lip as she sorted through the mechanics. "Why did he tell me he'd hurt Bethany if I didn't come out of my room? And why is Bethany sleeping like this?"

"I'm sure he didn't mean any harm," Layla replied.

She eyed the man. He seemed sympathetic, so she stepped close to him and took Bethany from his arms, cradling the girl tightly in her own. He let the child go without an objection.

"She's sleeping," he said. "Cried herself to sleep."

Layla nodded slowly. She hated to hear that Bethany went through such an ordeal, but she was glad her baby girl wasn't hurt.

"What's your name?" Layla asked the man. "So we know what to call you. If we're going to be together for a while today, we might as well call you by your name."

Layla's heart rate instantly slowed as she felt Bethany against her. Hailey returned to lean on her mother's side. Finally, Layla could speak without the cotton sensation in her mouth. Maybe they'd make it out of this predicament in one piece. She was still worried about Trent and she wondered what had happened to Tabby, but her girls were priority number one. Trent and Tabby could fend for themselves.

"Come on," Layla continued, half smiling at the man. "You know our names-- I'm Layla Grant, and this is Hailey and Bethany. It's only fair that you tell us yours."

"Okay, I will tell you," he replied. "But this doesn't mean we're friends. I'm here to do a job. Not here to make friends."

Layla nodded her understanding. Hailey furrowed her brow in confusion, but she stayed quiet and listened.

"My name is Mikhail," he said.

"Michael?" Hailey asked, to clarify.

"No, Mikhail," the man replied, enunciating this time.

He made exaggerated movements with his lips that would have been laughable, had the situation not been so tense. There was silence for a moment as his name sunk in.

"What's your last name?" Hailey asked sweetly.

"Semenov," Mikhail answered quickly.

"Same as Ivan's," Layla mumbled. "We met him in the driveway a while ago," she explained to Hailey.

Mikhail nodded. "Yes. Ivan is my brother."

Layla's brows raised. "So you understand the sibling bond and how important it is to keep these girls safe and together.

He nodded, albeit somewhat reluctantly. They were making slow but steady progress.

"Are you from a different country?" Hailey asked.

She twirled a strand of hair with one finger as she spoke. It was a good sign, as far as Layla was concerned. The girl was beginning to relax.

"I am from Russia," Mikhail said. "Like your mom and dad."

Layla's jaw dropped. She couldn't have hidden her reaction if she'd tried. The girls had no idea she and Trent were anything other than a normal American couple. How dare Mikhail spill the beans like this, exposing one of her deepest, darkest secrets?

"No they're not," Hailey replied. "My mom and dad are from California. Right here, in Rosemary Run."

Mikhail raised a finger in the air and made a tisk-tisk motion. "No, no. They are from Russia. Real names are Petra and Dmitriy. You have been told a lie, little one."

He leaned down toward Hailey when he said it.

Maybe it was for emphasis. Or maybe he didn't know what to do with his hands now that he was no longer holding Bethany. Either way, it startled the girl and took back the ease that had been building between them.

"That's not true," Hailey said. Then quietly, while staring up at her mother, "is it, Mama?"

7

OLD COUNTRY

Petra Ozlov was a name that Layla hadn't heard spoken in nearly fifteen years.

Mikhail had been telling the God's honest truth. It was her real name. She was from Russia, just as he'd said. He'd been right about Trent, too. Also from Russia, Trent's real name was Dmitriy Kozlov. And no one in America had the slightest idea. Especially not the Grant girls.

By the time Hailey and Bethany had come along, Layla and Trent had established themselves as normal Americans. They'd talked like Americans without a Russian accent, they'd dressed like Americans, and they'd maintained zero ties to their homeland. No ties, that is, other than the ones mandated by their chosen profession.

Communication with their superiors wasn't frequent. It was shrouded in secrecy at the highest levels. As a matter of practicality in their daily lives, Layla and Trent *were* regular Americans. Trent was in banking, and Layla was a stay-at-home wife and mom.

Period. End of story. No one knew the secrets they kept.

Layla winced as she looked into Hailey's big, trusting brown eyes. The little dear had a right to know. This was her family heritage, after all. And she deserved to understand where she came from.

On the other hand, Layla couldn't expect the girls to keep secrets this monumental. Other kids would ask. People in grocery stores would ask. When they got older, boyfriends would ask. It would be so hard for Hailey and Bethany to know the full, real story and then be expected not to tell anyone. It just wouldn't work. No way.

Layla decided right then and there, standing in the big doorway of her Rosemary Run bedroom-- that the girls couldn't know the truth. Not until they were much older. She'd have to find a way to unring the bell that Mikhail had rung. To find an explanation that would satisfy Hailey's curiosity while also keeping the child safe from the danger that the truth would bring. Not to mention, the impact the truth could have on Trent's court case and criminal conviction was something she had no choice but to consider.

Layla didn't even know those implications. Not really. But she knew that Trent's legal troubles would cause a rift with Mother Russia. He was supposed to be laying low in America, minding his business and acting normal until it was time to spring into action. They both were. That time had not yet come, but the exposure related to Trent's arrest hadn't been what their handlers had in mind.

"Shh," Layla breathed, leaning hard against Hailey while still cradling a sleeping Bethany in her arms. "Don't worry, honey. Mikhail has me confused with someone else. It's okay. I'm the same Mama you know and love."

If looks could kill, Mikhail would have been a dead man. Layla shot him the harshest, most threatening look she could muster. She was angry that he'd dared say what he had. And she wanted to make him pay. Her face burned red with the intent to stop this train in its tracks.

For his part, Mikhail just shrugged.

"I take it you don't have kids of your own?" Layla asked him.

The leather in his jacket crunched as he folded his arms over his chest. It was a defensive pose. Layla was glad to see that she was getting to him. He ought to feel bad for speaking so openly in front of the children.

"No, I do not have kids."

"That's obvious," she chided. "Look, Mikhail, I'm not sure who you have me confused with, but I'm from right here-- Rosemary Run, California-- just like my daughter says. I don't talk like you. I don't look like you. Russia sounds like a nice place to visit sometime, but I'm all American."

Hailey nodded emphatically, as if to reinforce her mother's assertion of proof. "Yeah," she muttered. The word came out muffled thanks to the barrier provided by Layla's skirt, but the sentiment was heard loud and clear.

Mikhail stared into Layla's eyes. He was deciding whether or not to push the issue. Maybe he was debating the pros and cons of insisting on the truth. Beads of perspiration formed on Layla's brow as she waited for him to let the subject drop. So much depended on his cooperation. She needed him to let this go. To let Hailey believe in the facade.

Layla quickly went over the basics in her mind. She felt bad lying to the girls. But it wasn't like their family was fake. Trent and Layla might not be their real names, yet that didn't matter one iota when it came to their very real love for each other and for their girls.

"Mikhail?" Layla tried. "Can we have a private conversation in the next room? I'll place the girls in my big bed while we step down the hall for a chat? Okay?"

He shrugged again. "Okay," he agreed. "Keep the bedroom door open so I can see them at all times. I have to keep an eye on the three of you."

"Okay, thank you," Layla agreed, then she took Hailey and Bethany to her and Trent's king-sized bed.

Layla resented the insertion into her family's Sunday routine. However, she knew she needed to focus on the positive and control the situation as much as possible. She appreciated what minor victories she could win.

Bethany stirred when she was moved, but soon settled back into a peaceful sleep beside her sister. Hailey was content to watch TV while Layla and Mikhail talked. Layla handed her the remote and she expertly navigated to a new episode of her favorite cartoon.

"Stay here," Layla said. "In the bed. We have to be able to see you."

"I know, Mama," Hailey replied. "I'll do a good job."

Layla kissed the top of Bethany's head, then Hailey's. "I know you will," she said quietly. "Try not to be afraid."

Hailey nodded.

Layla returned to where Mikhail was waiting, then

motioned for him to follow her down the long hall and away from the girls' earshot. When they reached the far end of the open space, Layla stopped and turned to face the big man who had dropped a bomb on her carefully constructed family life. It was hard not to be seething mad at him. It took every ounce of Layla's restraint to remain cordial.

"What?" he asked simply.

Mikhail was, apparently, a man of few words.

"Why would you do that?" Layla implored.

She kept her mouth turned away from the master bedroom to be sure Hailey wouldn't read her lips.

Mikhail shrugged. "I was just speaking the truth. What's so bad about that?"

"Our girls don't know the truth," Layla replied. "And if Trent-- *Dmitriy*-- and I are to keep our identities under cover, we must be sure the girls stay uninformed. Think it through. These kinds of secrets are too massive for young kids to keep. The girls are five and seven. *Far* too young for international espionage."

"Huh," he grunted. "You've changed."

"What are you talking about?" Layla asked, a scowl on her face. "I don't know you."

"Oh, but you do," Mikhail replied. "Are you going to tell me you don't remember?"

Layla squinted her eyes and pursed her lips, struggling to jog her memory. Mikhail and Ivan were vaguely familiar. She tried picturing Mikhail as a young man with hair and a lankier build. It took a minute, then suddenly, it dawned on her.

"Wait! Are you the Semenov brothers who lived near

the pub in my village? The one at the very edge of town, near the forest leading to the Black Sea?"

"That's the one. Our father owns the pub, called Alexi's. He is Alexi! The old goat is still going strong at sixty-five. He doesn't look a day over forty."

Mikhail smiled as he spoke about his father and the pub. His enthusiasm was contagious. It immediately made Layla smile, too.

"I remember Alexi's!" Layla exclaimed, excited by the connection. "I haven't thought about it in years, but I remember. There were large copper tiles on the ceiling inside, and outside, there was a wooden statue of a bear on its hind legs, right? Oh, and they served burgers on a wooden plate with bark around the edges... like a real slice of a tree trunk."

"Yes, good memory," Mikhail said. "Those *were* real slices of tree trunk, sealed for use as serving trays. We cater to skiers who come to town for the woods and the slopes... lyzhnyy sklon."

Layla smiled, the Russian translation tickling her ears in a delightful way.

She and Trent rarely spoke Russian to each other anymore. They rarely spoke Russian at all, for that matter. They'd been told it would be best to immerse themselves in American culture and to forget that of their homeland. Only Layla couldn't forget. Not completely. Mikhail and Ivan were bringing it all back, in living color.

"You're a lot nicer than your brother," Layla mused. "What crawled up his butt and died?"

Mikhail waved a hand in the air. "He's more intense

than I am. We need him to be that way... to be in charge. Inside, though, he's a big softie."

"It didn't seem that way when I met him earlier. He would hardly let me speak. Every time I opened my mouth, it seemed, he threw a hand up to silence me," Layla explained.

"He's on a mission. Forgive him. We all have our part to do. You understand," Mikhail said.

"I don't know," Layla replied. "Do I?"

"You should," he said, lowering one brow for emphasis. "I see that you have become a good mother. But you must remember why you're here. Have you forgotten, Petra?"

She shook her head, turning briefly to check on the girls. They were still in bed, Bethany sleeping and Hailey gazing up at the television.

"No, I haven't," Layla replied, holding back the urge to correct the name. "I could never forget. But becoming a mother has changed me. I don't know. Maybe time has changed me, too. If I had to do it all over again…"

"Don't say that," Mikhail interrupted. "Don't you dare."

Layla sighed. "Yeah, I know."

She did know. All too well. Those who disobeyed their handlers or tried to defect were punished harshly. Typically, by death. There was no path for changing one's mind in this situation. Once a Russian operative, always a Russian operative. At least, as far as Layla and Trent knew.

The Grants-- actually the Kozlovs-- were supposed to be sleeper agents, inserted into the United States long-term to blend in and live normal lives until the day they were needed by their country. Should that day arrive, they'll be expected to follow orders to the letter.

"Why are you here?" Layla asked Mikhail. "With your strange, angular car and your black leather, and your... I don't know. All of this. Is it for show? Are you assassins now or something?"

They were loaded questions with answers Layla didn't really want to learn. Yet she had to. She had to know what she and her family were facing if there was any chance of getting the girls through this nightmare unscathed.

She wished her girls were older. Teenagers, at least, would be better able to fend for themselves if both of their parents had to... go away.

"Do you really want to know?" Mikhail replied.

"Yes. Whether I want to or not, I must know. Please, tell me."

PART II

IDENTITY CRISIS

8

FORK IN THE ROAD

"Hello?" Layla said politely as she answered the landline phone in the living room.

She sat on an easy chair and thumbed the seam absentmindedly as she waited to hear who was calling. She hoped it might be her husband.

It had been nearly forty-eight hours since Trent and Ivan had disappeared for a little talk.

Mikhail had stayed and-- as promised-- had kept an eye on Layla and the girls at all times. He'd been pleasant, for the most part, even joking around with Hailey and Bethany and having won them over to some extent. Yet the intrusion was growing tiresome, to say the least.

Layla hadn't asked Mikhail about her frantic 9-1-1 call to the local police the day he and Ivan had arrived. She wondered what had happened to Officer Rucker and his proclamation that officers had been on their way.

She also hadn't mentioned Tabby's whereabouts, too frightened to learn the answers to the nagging questions about her friend that had kept her awake at night.

Layla had a sinking feeling that Tabby had found herself in harm's way. The woman hadn't called or texted, despite Layla's repeated voicemail pleas for a response. Layla wasn't sure she could handle knowing exactly what had happened. It wasn't like Tabby to drop out of sight like this. Especially not when she knew the peril the Grant family faced. She'd been there to see it for herself. She'd met Ivan-- and presumably Mikhail, too-- in the flesh.

The phone line sat dead. "Hello? Is anybody there?" Layla tried again.

"Oh, yes," a man's voice replied. "Sorry. I didn't know anyone had picked up. Is Mr. Grant available?"

"He's not here right now. May I take a message?" Layla asked.

She kept her tone light and airy. It seemed the only thing to do.

Mikhail entered the room to see what Layla was up to. He was becoming kinder and gentler the longer he hung around the Grant girls, but like he'd said, he had a job to do. They all did. Anything he learned about Layla and Trent's private business could be used against them once shared with Ivan. Layla was well aware of the risks.

"Um… well…" the man on the other end of the line stammered. "I don't know if I should…"

"If you should leave a message?" Layla asked, finishing his thought.

"That's right. Unfortunately, it's a sensitive matter," the man said softly.

"Not too sensitive for his wife, I hope," Layla said.

Her voice was growing strained. She desperately wanted to know what this man did. Perhaps he knew where Trent was. If so, she owed it to her family to find out.

She shifted in the chair, turning her back to Mikhail as if that would somehow erase his presence.

Romeo groaned from his spot on the floor across from Layla, disturbed by her phone call that was interrupting his nap. The dog had grown accustomed to Mikhail's presence and had gone back to his usual lazy bones status.

"May I ask who's calling?" Layla tried.

There was a pause on the other end of the line. Silence filled the space between them for what felt like an uncomfortably long time. Finally, the man spoke.

"It's Fred Lowell. I'm Mr. Grant's criminal defense attorney."

Layla's brows shot up. She had heard the man's name when Trent first hired him. She hadn't spoken to him yet, though.

Fred Lowell had a reputation for being one of the best in Northern California. Maybe even one of the best in the nation. He'd won many cases for clients when it had looked like the odds were stacked against them. On top of that, he had a reputation for being an ethical man. That was nearly unheard of for an individual in his position.

Trent had chosen to keep a separation between his criminal case and his family, to be extra careful that Layla didn't get wrapped up in anything that could jeopardize her good name and clean record. He'd wanted to be meticulous in his planning for the next phase of their lives. Layla appreciated that more than she could adequately express.

Someone had to stick around and take good care of their little girls.

"I've heard of you," Layla replied slowly. "How can I help?"

Mikhail stepped closer, moving around so that he could make eye contact with Layla. "Who is it?" he mouthed.

Layla waved him away, then turned the other way in her chair, her attention focused on Fred. Mikhail sighed and teetered on his feet. He was growing impatient.

The girls were coloring at the dining room table. They hadn't been paying much attention when the phone first rang, but thanks to Mikhail's antics they, too, were listening to Layla's every word like little hawks.

"I'm sorry to bother you," Fred said. "It's just that I haven't heard from your husband in a few days. He was supposed to come into my office yesterday so that I could prepare him for his court date coming up. It's helpful if I run clients through a few mock sessions before they face the real thing."

"Um hmm," Layla replied, listening.

"I assume you know about his upcoming court appearance?"

"I do," she confirmed.

Mikhail stepped closer, getting in her face. "Who?" he mouthed again, snapping his thick fingers this time for emphasis.

To Layla's credit, she was aware that Mikhail didn't want his presence known. In what had become a tight-rope balancing act between various evils in her life, she was right in the fact that she had the upper hand as long as Mikhail thought he'd be exposed. In that regard, Fred's call had been a Godsend.

"So, is everything alright?" the attorney asked.

"No," she said simply.

Mikhail seemed to sense the violation. He tensed, his hands balling into fists at his sides. Layla knew she had to throw him off the scent, and fast.

"Do you represent Moe Griffith?" she asked politely.

Layla was partially curious about Trent's colleague at the bank, but she also needed to change the subject to appease Mikhail.

She couldn't have her new overseer getting suspicious and ratting her out to his meaner big brother. That could spell even more trouble for Trent. Layla suspected that Mikhail couldn't hurt her or the girls. She wasn't positive, though. She didn't want to risk it and find out she was wrong. Not about something as important as their physical safety.

"I don't," Fred replied. "I'm not sure who is representing Mr. Griffith. Last I heard, it was a TV lawyer from Los Angeles who represents celebrities in high profile cases. Moe's history as a player in the NFL gives him a certain notoriety."

"Is it Gloria Allred?" Layla asked. "I've heard of her representing celebrities, although I think she just likes the attention for herself. I've seen her all over the television."

Mikhail cocked his head to one side as he tried to figure out what Layla was talking about.

"No," Fred said. "Ms. Allred handles mostly women's rights issues. She wouldn't be the right fit for Mr. Griffith. Why do you ask?"

"Just curious," Layla replied.

Fred hadn't asked about Layla's indication that everything wasn't okay. He'd noted her response, though.

"Ms. Grant," he said, "it seems like something is off here. This is the first time we've spoken, but I get the idea you're in some kind of trouble. Is there someone I can call to help you?"

Layla sighed heavily. She so wanted to say yes. To have him check on Tabby. To have him send a search party after her husband. To get the local police involved. Maybe the FBI or Homeland Security or the CIA, even.

This was big. If the U.S. government had any idea what was going on between the Grants and the Semenov brothers, they'd send someone. That much was certain.

At the heart of it, Layla wanted the protection offered to every American. She wanted to *be* American. A real American citizen who belongs in the country and has equal and inalienable rights. Like her daughters. Since Fred was a protector of the law, sort of, a part of Layla thought maybe he could protect her rights.

It seemed silly given the enormity of her obligations to her home country, but deep inside, Layla began to wonder if she actually could defect. Could America protect her?

"Ms. Grant? Are you still there?" Fred asked, the concern evident in his voice.

Layla didn't respond. She sat, still as a church mouse, waiting for the cat who wanted to toy with her to look the other way.

They could be tapping her phone, for all she knew. No means of communication was safe at this point. Maybe it never was.

Hailey noticed her mother's distress and called to her from the dining room table. "Mama, who are you talking to?" she asked.

The child's voice was enough to snap Layla out of it. She'd been staring at an empty spot on the wall, but Hailey's voice brought her back to reality.

Layla put a hand over the receiver so as not to yell in Fred's ear. "A friend of your dad's," she explained.

She knew the girls would catch on soon enough.

"Is he traveling with Daddy now?" Hailey tried. "Can I talk to him?"

Layla's face scrunched into a knot. "What? No, Daddy isn't with him. Give me a few minutes. I'll be right there."

Hailey's shoulders slumped. She'd been excited at the fleeting prospect of being able to talk with her father. She remained at the table, though, moving her crayons begrudgingly. The poor little thing.

Layla had told the girls Trent was out of town for work the past two days. What else was she supposed to tell them? If Trent was soon sentenced to federal prison, she'd have to tell them he'd be out of town for a very long time. Maybe years. Maybe decades. Of course, she wouldn't be able to keep the charade going forever. Hailey and Bethany would be too old for that at some point. They weren't there now, though. For now, Layla wanted to protect their innocence.

The girls had a slew of questions about the family's current situation. Namely, they wanted to know why they'd had to go to their rooms and hide the day the Semenov brothers arrived. Then they'd wanted to know why Mikhail had scared Bethany so badly that the girl had exhausted herself crying. They wanted to know where their daddy was, when he was coming back, and why in the world Mikhail was staying in their house and watching their every move.

None of it made sense to little girls who had-- until now-- lived normal, peaceful lives with loving parents. Layla was working overtime to keep up. It was proving difficult to keep the girls calm and reassured while also handling Mikhail and her own anxiety about the danger at hand.

Fred's call was complicating matters. It would probably be easiest and smartest to brush him off and convince him that everything was fine and dandy. Layla had practice acting. It was part of her job and her life, after all. She could have convinced Fred there was nothing to worry about. But she didn't want to. She began to suspect that she'd need the man's help if she wanted to save her family.

"Sorry," Layla said into the phone. "I'm here. What were you saying?"

Mikhail eyed her. He wanted to know who she was talking to, and he was tired of waiting.

"Someone is there. Someone you're afraid of," Fred said softly.

Layla's pulse quickened as she debated how to respond. This could be her chance. Or it could be her downfall.

She wasn't sure what to do.

9

BECOMING

By the time day three rolled around, Layla was beginning to feel like a prisoner in her own home. Trent's sudden departure had caused a major upheaval in their lives.

Mikhail had been breathing down their necks, keeping an even closer eye on Layla and the girls ever since her telephone conversation with Fred.

She'd almost asked the old man for help but had decided against it at the last minute. Instead, she'd hung up the phone without saying goodbye. Layla had feared her captor would grow meaner and less forgiving if she'd told Fred that she and the girls were in trouble. Her relationship with Mikhail had vacillated from that of old childhood friends to jailer and his detainee.

"You stink," Layla said to Mikhail as she turned her nose up at him.

The big man sat perched on a stool near the kitchen island eating a microwaved breakfast burrito.

The prior evening, Mikhail had ordered some food

from Harmon's Grocery and had it delivered. It had struck Layla as a little strange the way he'd insisted on supporting a local family business instead of buying from a big chain store, but when he'd asked, she'd recommended Harmon's. The family grocery had recently reopened after a devastating fire.

Mikhail had taken care of their need for sustenance. His order hadn't been what Layla and the girls usually ate. They had some supplies when this ordeal started, though, so they were getting by.

Unfortunately for those within smelling distance, though, Mikhail hadn't bathed. He didn't seem to have a change of clothes, and he presumably couldn't take his eyes off of the Grants for long enough to get cleaned up.

"Yeah, so?" he replied as he chewed, his mouth packed with burrito.

"So, you need a shower. This is only going to get worse. Your stink, that is. I don't want to smell it," Layla chided.

Mikhail stopped chewing long enough to lift one arm and take a deep whiff of his pit. "Oh, God," he said, wrinkling his face. "That's bad."

"See? What did I tell you?"

The girls were upstairs, playing in Hailey's room. Layla had calculated her move and had chosen to approach Mikhail about a shower when they weren't around. Even Romeo was upstairs with the kids. Layla and her childhood acquaintance were the only two people in the room.

"I don't have any luggage," Mikhail said, gesturing

upstairs as if he was a welcomed guest in the Grant home. "No clean clothes."

"You could wear some of Trent's," Layla offered. "They might be small, but they'll do."

"Might be small?" Mikhail asked with a laugh.

They both knew that he was a much larger man than Trent. It wasn't even close.

Layla proceeded, determined to get the man to wash and hopeful that his shower would buy her a few precious moments of privacy to make another phone call.

"I can give you a big tshirt and a pair of athletic shorts. They'll work long enough for me to wash and dry the clothes you're wearing," she explained.

He looked at her skeptically as he continued to chew, wolfing down the burrito. He didn't say no. That was a good sign.

"And what will you do while I take this shower?" he asked.

Layla smiled. "What I just told you. I'll put your dirty clothes in the washer."

"What else?"

"Come on," she urged. "We've spent the last three days together. I don't know about you, but I have no idea how much longer we'll be here. I don't want to smell your b.o. any more. You seriously stink. Badly."

Mikhail had let Layla and the girls bathe. He'd waited outside the bathrooms each day while they'd moved through their usual routines. Yet he'd been too afraid to leave Layla unattended on the other side of the bathroom door.

"How can I be sure you'll stay? Without causing trouble?" he asked.

Layla looked him directly in the eye as she formulated a response. It was crucial that she didn't act scared of him, even though she was.

"Am I your prisoner?" she asked pointedly. "Because I thought I was your colleague."

He laughed while finishing the last bite of burrito and wiping the corners of his mouth with a paper napkin.

"That's a good question," he said with a chuckle. "You tell me. You should be my colleague. That's what you're supposed to be. I'm not sure where your head is."

Layla scoffed. "My head is with my little girls," she replied. "I wouldn't do anything to put them in danger. I understand that you were ordered to watch me until Ivan and Trent return. And I can-- theoretically-- understand why our superiors might wonder if my loyalties still lie with Mother Russia. It's been a long time since I've been in contact with any of them. But I promise you, those girls are my priority."

"You're talking in circles, just like you were taught," Mikhail said.

"How so?"

"All the talk about your girls, but you might turn around and say you had to run away to protect them," he continued.

"Run?" Layla asked. "From the Russian government? From the Federal Security Service? How would one do that, exactly?"

"You're right," Mikhail replied. "There is nowhere to

run. Our reach is too far. Our power is too great. Your only choice is to cooperate. You swore an oath."

Layla had sworn an oath. Trent had, too. She knew it would be an uphill battle if she decided to defect from her country of origin. She wasn't sure if Mikhail was aware of her divided loyalties, but she was thinking about various options to try.

"I certainly did," she confirmed. "I was a younger woman then."

"A woman without American little girls," Mikhail added, finishing her thought.

"That's true," Layla admitted.

There was a moment of silence between them. They each looked at the other, contemplating the enormity of Layla's situation.

For Mikhail's part, he could see both sides. "I never married," he said, breaking the silence. "I'd like to have a family of my own someday. It hasn't been the right time yet."

"Has there been the right woman?" Layla asked, grateful that he was opening up.

That had to be good for her. It meant that he had compassion for Layla and the girls. Layla hoped it might mean that he'd set them free at some point, if the circumstances were suitable.

"There was a woman," Mikhail replied. "Or I should say there *is* a woman?"

Layla smiled, taking a stool and dragging it around the island across from him, then sitting down. "Oh? In Russia?"

He nodded. "In Sochi. Very near to our village."

Hearing the name of Sochi brought back a rush of memories. The resort town on the Black Sea was less than an hour from the village where Layla had grown up. It was breathtakingly beautiful there, all green mountains and blue sea. The architecture was stunning, too.

"Ah, Sochi," she said with an even bigger smile. "What beauty. People tend to think of our country as either Moscow or a frozen tundra, but it's so much more."

"Breathtaking," Mikhail agreed.

"Is your woman breathtaking, too?"

He nodded again. "She sure took my breath away. We loved each other once."

The way he said it made Layla sad for him. "Why not now?" she asked. "What came between the two of you?"

Layla was sort of surprised that Mikhail was being so open with her. She wondered if it was an act. It didn't seem like it, though. She could see the emotion all over his face when he talked about his lost love.

He gestured into the air and spun one finger around, apparently, to indicate that his career had overtaken every other aspect of his life.

"Work problems?" Layla asked.

"You could say that," he confirmed. "I wanted a family. I *did*. It wasn't meant to be. This job is... all encompassing."

Layla raised an eyebrow in agreement. "You can say that again. I'm not sure I would have had children if I hadn't been ordered to."

"You were ordered to have children?"

She nodded. "Trent-- Dmitriy-- and I weren't married when we were first assigned here. We were engaged to be married and they liked that we were a real couple. But we didn't get married until a few years later. The ceremony was here, in California. Like real Americans."

"And then they ordered you to have children?" Mikhail repeated.

Layla smiled. "They did. We didn't mind, at that point. We were enjoying our new lives. We loved each other deeply, and we wanted a family."

"You said you might not have had them…"

"If I were a single person, or in a more active role like yours," Layla explained. "You are in a more active role, aren't you? I mean, other than Trent's legal trouble-- which, granted, is a big deal-- my most pressing concern is shopping for the girls' school clothes and supplies before they start a new school year in a couple of weeks."

"My role is more active than that, yes," Mikhail confirmed.

Layla paused as she thought it over from his point of view. "I guess you might have liked an assignment like mine… with your love?"

He nodded, slowly and mournfully. "I might have liked that."

"I'm sorry," she said.

He looked at her quizzically. "Why are you sorry? You didn't do anything wrong. It isn't your fault."

"Oh, it's just something Americans say when they feel bad for you. I mean that I'm sorry you're sad. I wish you weren't."

"I see," he replied. "The English language has so many exceptions. And the colloquial phrases in America are a challenge to keep up with."

Layla laughed. "I completely agree with you. Your English is good, though."

"Yeah?" he asked.

"Yeah."

Layla rubbed a thumb along the edge of the counter as she worked even harder to consider Mikhail's perspective. She thought that maybe she could make friends with him. If they could develop a real friendship built on trust, maybe he would help her.

"Hey, I'll tell you a funny story about me when I was new in this country and learning all the silly American slang that people around here use."

"Okay." He smiled at her. It was a genuine, friendly smile. "Go ahead."

"I was at a picnic hosted by the bank Trent works at. It was summer, and the potato salad must have been out in the sun too long because it made me sick."

"Food poisoning?"

"I think so," I said, continuing. "I was queasy and holding one hand over my stomach. Someone asked if I wasn't feeling well and I told them that I thought I might toss some cookies. Get it? Toss *some* cookies?"

He obviously didn't get it. Layla didn't blame him.

"What does that mean?" he asked, perplexed.

"I didn't know either," she explained. "I thought I had it right, but the look on the woman's face told me I'd missed the mark. The phrase is 'toss your cookies' when you think you may vomit. By using the word some instead of the word my, it came out sounding very strange."

"Okay, I see."

"So, toss some cookies sounded like I should be throwing cookies…"

They laughed together over the absurdity of it all, although Layla wasn't sure Mikhail ever came to understand the subtle differences in the phrase.

"If only we could speak our native tongue around here," Mikhail mused.

Layla nodded. "It would have been nice."

Silence filled the room again, and they stared at each other, both unsure as to what they were becoming. After what felt like a long while, Layla spoke.

"Are we bonding?" she asked. "Could we be friends?"

Mikhail hesitated to reply, although he couldn't help but smile. "I'm not positive," he said. "But I'd like to take that shower."

10

TICKING CLOCK

As promised, Layla found some of Trent's athletic clothes that were baggy enough to strap around Mikhail. Acting as a good host, she set out a fresh bar of soap, a towel and washcloth, and a brand new toiletry kit complete with travel-sized deodorant, toothbrush, toothpaste, and comb. She showed her guest to the downstairs bathroom. It adjoined a spare bedroom and was rarely used.

If Mikhail hadn't been so bent on watching Layla's every move, he could have been enjoying his own guest suite the whole time.

"I won't stink any longer," he said, gripping the clean bath towel in one hand and the clean clothes in the other.

"At least, not for a day or two," Layla said jokingly.

She wanted to ask how long he planned to stay and how long her husband would be away, but she didn't dare rock the boat. She was making progress. A few days ago, she'd been terrified that he was going to hurt Bethany. Today, they were chatting like old friends.

"Thank you for your hospitality," Mikhail said.

He went into the bathroom, closed the door, and turned on the water in the shower. The sound made Layla's heart race. She knew she had a very short time to do what she must.

"You're welcome," she called back, all the while plotting her next move.

What's next?

She talked through the options in her mind, quickly debating and dismissing the riskier ones. She decided this was a long game and that she had better be subtle and calculated to avoid tipping Mikhail and his brother off.

Stepping as quietly as she could manage through the downstairs, she made her way to Trent's old exercise room that had recently been converted into an art studio for the girls. If she remembered correctly, there was a box of old cell phones in the back of the closet. If she could find one with enough power, she could connect via wifi and make an outgoing call. She'd need to move quickly so as not to get caught by Mikhail when he came out of the bathroom.

Layla estimated that she had approximately five minutes to find the phone, power it up, make the call, and get back to the living room as if nothing had happened.

She turned on the television in the living room as she scooted through. She'd pretend she was casually watching the news. Or whatever came on when she powered the thing up. She didn't have time to surf through the channels.

"Hailey? Bethany?" she called up the stairs as she walked by.

"Yes?" they replied in unison.

"I'm watching a little TV while Mikhail gets a shower, okay? You can keep playing up there until lunch time."

"Okay, Mama!" and "Good!" sounded from their location.

Satisfied that the girls wouldn't come downstairs and get mixed up in what Layla was about to do, she hurriedly found the box of old phones and got one to work with wifi.

Come on, come on, she thought as she dialed the number and waited for the call to connect. Thanks to an old caller ID readout on the landline phone, Layla had memorized the phone number after the call had come in the day before.

The old man answered right away.

"Fred?" Layla whispered into the phone. "Are you there?"

"Ms. Grant," he said.

She didn't let him waste any time.

"This is extremely urgent and I only have a minute. Listen carefully."

"Go ahead," he said, the sounds of a paper and pen clanking around on a hard surface in the background.

Layla took a deep breath, hoping she was doing the right thing.

"I don't have time to sugar coat this. Trent and I are Russian nationals placed in the United States as sleeper agents. We hadn't been in contact with our handlers for many years, but they're here now and Trent went with one of them. Another one is staying at the house with me and the girls."

"I see," Fred replied in a monotone voice. He didn't seem phased by this information.

"I don't know about Trent, but I have the girls to think about," she continued. "I want to defect. I am prepared to give up allegiance to Russia and pledge allegiance to the United States. Can you make contact with someone in your government for me?"

"I'm not sure--"

"Try," she said. "Please! I need to keep my girls safe. I'll do anything that's asked of me. But I have to go now. I'll try to call you again sometime soon."

"Wait!" Fred shouted. The exclamation was surprisingly loud compared to everything else he'd said. "What is your real name? I'll need to know if I'm to convince authorities that you're legitimate."

Layla sighed. This was the part that sealed the deal. There would be no going back once she revealed her real name.

"Petra Ozlov," she said. "From a small village near Sochi."

"And Trent's real name?"

Layla shook her head, then glanced at the doorway. She thought she could still hear the shower running, but she was too far away to tell for sure. The din of the television provided a sound buffer that was both beneficial for her and possibly not, depending on how fast Mikhail moved through the shower.

"I'm not sure he wants to defect," she replied. "I wish for him to be with the girls and me. Our love is real. But I can't speak for him."

"Ms. Grant," Fred said. "I have information from your

husband that leads me to believe that he does, in fact, wish to pledge allegiance to the United States as well. Please, tell me his name if you want me to help you."

A drawer slammed from what really sounded like the guest bathroom and Layla knew she was out of time. She didn't have time to debate whether or not to provide her husband's real name. On a whim and with the wish that the family could somehow stay together, she revealed the truth.

"Dmitriy Kozlov," she said. "Now I have to go. God help us all."

Layla ended the call, then turned the phone off and stuffed it back into the box with the others like it. She was careful to maneuver it all the way to the bottom of the box so it wouldn't be the first one someone would pick up should they follow her tracks. Grateful that Trent hadn't thrown the box of old phones away like she'd asked him to, she closed the closet then returned to the living room to plop down in front of the TV. She focused all of her attention on the news program, and just in time, too. Mikhail exited the bathroom less than a minute after she'd hit the sofa.

"Miss me?" he joked.

His bald head was still wet. He looked strange in Trent's clothes, but he didn't look bad. Just different.

"Hardly time to miss you with all the togetherness of late," she replied.

"Yeah, well, you might miss me when I'm gone."

"When do you think that will be, exactly?" she asked in the friendliest tone she could muster. "I'd like to know when I can expect my husband."

Mikhail shrugged. "I told you before. I don't know. I have to wait until Ivan updates me. He'll call when he's ready."

Layla sighed. "I get that, but Trent is due in court next week. Does Ivan know that? He could be in lots of trouble if he doesn't appear in front of the judge."

"Ivan knows. What do you think they're talking about?"

Layla moved forward to the edge of her seat. This was news. "Wait. You know what they're talking about? And you haven't told me, all this time?"

"I know some things. Sort of."

"What do you mean?" she asked. "What does Ivan want with Trent?"

Mikhail sat down on the easy chair next to the landline phone. The same one Layla had sat on when she spoke with Fred yesterday. For some reason, Mikhail's seating arrangement made her nervous. She wondered if it was some kind of sign. Could he know that she'd reached out to Fred for help? Surely not.

She told herself to get it together.

"You're asking the wrong question," Mikhail said as he leaned back in the chair and laced his hands above his head. "Ask me a different one."

Layla scowled. She wasn't in any mood to play games. If Mikhail knew something he was willing to share, she wished he would come right out and say it.

"I don't know what you want me to ask," Layla said. "I'd like to know what's going on. For my girls, you know. I mean, Mikhail, imagine for a moment that you were in my shoes, with kids who depended on you to keep them safe and provide them with a good life. I just want to know whatever it is I need to."

He nodded, this sentiment seeming to get to him. "Okay, then, imagine you're the Russian government and you learn that one of your assets is going to prison for a matter unrelated to the work he's been trained to do for you. What are the options?"

Layla moved even further forward on the edge of her seat, intrigued by the opportunity to dialogue like this. Maybe she would learn something useful.

"I suppose one option is to remove the asset from the country he's embedded in. So, in this case, that would mean returning Trent-- Dmitriy to Russia," she tried.

Mikhail hesitated before responding, but finally nodded his head. "That's one option, yes. And another?"

"Well, Russia could stay out of it and let things play out as they otherwise would…"

"Not that one," Mikhail replied quickly.

"Yeah, that would have been too easy," Layla agreed.

She just wanted an exit plan. A way to live a normal life with her husband and children. Why did it have to be so hard?

Mikhail watched Layla as she contemplated the options.

"Did he do it?" he asked.

"What?" Layla replied, unsure what Mikhail meant.

"The bank fraud. Is he guilty?"

She shook her head. "I don't believe so. He says he isn't, anyway. A colleague of his, Moe Griffith, has been charged with the same crimes. Trent thinks this is a smear campaign with Moe as the target. Trent just got caught in the crosshairs."

"That's unfortunate," Mikhail replied. "Although, it presents a certain opportunity for Russia, does it not?"

Layla cocked her head to one side. "To gain access to someone inside the prison system?"

Mikhail nodded. "Now you're getting there. So, we are presented with a choice."

"Go back to Russia or be an active foreign asset in federal prison?" Layla reiterated as the reality hit her like a lead weight.

Either way, her husband was going away. And either way, his life would be in far more danger than it had been up until now. He'd be a target in prison if anyone even suspected he was working for Russia. If he went home to Russia, he could be executed for failing to complete his mission.

Poor Trent. He was a good man. A family man. Parenthood had changed him, too. If she had it to do over again, she never would have agreed to be a Russian agent. How foolish she'd been.

"That's right, essentially," Mikhail confirmed. "The decision is taking longer than expected."

Layla nodded, shifting her weight back and leaning against the cushion behind her. "What will happen to me and the girls?"

"I don't know for sure," he replied. "You might be sent back to Russia. Or you might stay here, to wait for your husband to return home from prison."

11

TIME MARCHES ON

"Mama?" Bethany called from the top of the stairs. "I want to go out to a restaurant. A fancy one where we sit down and a waitress brings things to us."

It was day four since Trent's departure and they were going more than a little stir crazy. The afternoon was nearly over and dinner time would be arriving very soon.

"I know, honey," Layla replied. "We've been cooped up for a while now."

Mikhail nodded his agreement from the easy chair near the telephone. It was becoming his favorite spot in the house.

Bethany and Hailey trotted down the stairs cheerfully, determined to convince their mom to take them into town. Layla was reading a novel while resting on the couch. It seemed silly to read at a time like this, but all there was to do was to wait.

"Can we go?" Hailey asked, echoing her little sister's

plea. "I feel like eating at Brick House Cafe. I know it's one of your favorites, Mama."

Layla smiled. Brick House Cafe was indeed one of her favorites.

The locally-owned establishment was located in Rosemary Run's quaint downtown. Layla often liked to take an after-dinner stroll past the nearby shops when she ate there. Not to mention, the exposed-brick walls and city-village vibe had always appealed to her.

The cafe had been built into the brick of a taller building and featured large windows around the front three sides. It reminded Layla a lot of the architecture back in her Russian village, which gave her an idea. Maybe if she pitched it to Mikhail that way, he'd allow them to venture out for a meal.

"I don't know," Layla replied. "Mikhail, what do you say? The place Hailey's talking about is a lot like Alexi's. I'd love for you to see it."

"What's Alexi's?" Hailey asked innocently.

"It's a restaurant in the mountains that Mikhail and I have both been to," she replied. "It's one of his *favorite* restaurants." She turned her attention to Mikhail and used her best puppy-dog eyes. "Right?"

He took a deep breath. He had showered again that day and was feeling good. The four of them had grown comfortable with each other. Layla had even washed Mikhail's clothes, so they were ready to wear when he chose to put them on again. He was again borrowing some of Trent's old athletic items.

"I don't think..." he began.

"Don't say no," Layla interrupted, raising a hand in the air much like Ivan had done to her a few days prior. "It would do us all good to get out for a while."

That much was true. Although, what Layla really hoped for was a chance to get away from Mikhail. She wasn't sure what she'd do if she and the girls made it that far, but she wanted to try. Maybe they'd run into someone at the cafe who could help.

It was strange. She was comfortable with Mikhail and even felt like she could trust him, to some extent. Yet she also knew that she had to get away. No matter how sympathetic he felt toward her and the girls, he would probably follow his brother's orders to their detriment if forced to choose.

"Say yes, Micky-Hail!" Bethany chirped. "I'm hungry for a good, hot meal."

They all laughed at the little girl's pronunciation of his name and her wording. She must have heard something about a good, hot meal on a commercial or from an adult. It sounded too gimmicky for a five-year-old to come up with on their own.

"You silly goose," Layla said as she pulled Bethany into her arms. "I cook you good, hot meals all the time."

"No offense, Mama," Hailey added. "The food at restaurants is usually better than what you cook. That's why daddy likes to go out to eat."

Layla opened her mouth in mock outrage. "Seriously?" she asked. "Is that how you're going to do me? I thought you and Daddy liked my cooking. Wait until I tell him that I know how he really feels."

Mikhail laughed along with them. Layla could tell he was considering the restaurant idea.

"Who would we say I am when people ask? Because surely, someone would," he said. "In my experience, small town people are nosy."

Layla thought for a moment. She didn't want to teach the girls that it was okay to lie. These were unusual circumstances, though. And besides, it could be said that her entire life in America was a lie. What was one more, if it was intended to make things easier?

"You're my daddy's friend from his work," Bethany inserted before Layla had a chance to reply.

Bethany had become much more talkative and friendly with Mikhail in recent days. It was almost like she had forgotten how badly he had scared her when he'd first arrived.

"People may think I'm your mom's… *special…* friend unless we say otherwise," Mikhail replied. "I don't know how it is around here, but in general, people like to jump to conclusions. They talk."

Layla nodded. "That's true," she admitted. "I've spent years trying to keep up appearances and look like the perfect American family here in Rosemary Run. It's exhausting, and it never ends. If I bring you to dinner at Brick House Cafe without a good explanation of who you are, tongues will be wagging all over town."

Hailey and Bethany didn't quite catch the undertones, but Mikhail and Layla were communicating with each other loud and clear. For a hired gun, he was remarkably respectful. He didn't intend to impose on Trent's marriage or family. He hadn't acted inappropriately with Layla at any point during his stay.

"What if we say I'm your cousin? From out of town?" he asked Layla.

"But that isn't true!" Hailey proclaimed forcefully. "Mama and Daddy say we should always tell the truth. Always, always."

The girl clasped her hands in front of her chest as she said it. Her eyes were wide with concern.

"Yeah!" Bethany added in support of her big sister.

She struck a similar pose, hands clasped together.

Layla sighed. She hated the predicament she found herself in as a parent. She wanted to keep the good mothering she'd prided herself on going strong, yet she needed to try angles that might help her family out of this mess. Getting herself in public where she could potentially make a plea for help seemed worth the expense of a little white lie.

"You're right, Hailey, honey," she said. "It isn't good to lie… usually. But in this case, people might think something funny is going on if we tell them that Mikhail is staying with us. It's better to tell them that he's my cousin. It's none of their business, anyway. It's just something to tell them so they'll leave us alone."

The girls looked up at Layla with trusting eyes that seemed to peer right through her soul. They knew that something funny was going on. No one had to tell them. They saw it for themselves. They might not have been able to articulate exactly what they saw, but they knew something was very wrong.

"I know this is hard to understand," she continued. "But if we want to go out to dinner with Mikhail, I need you to trust me. We'll have to pretend he's my cousin. It's the only way."

"From out of town," Hailey added.

"That's right. Can you do that?" Layla asked. "Can you pretend with me?"

The girls looked at each other, then nodded reluctantly. "Okay, Mama," Hailey said. "We'll do what you ask."

"Good girl," Layla said, though she hated it. "It's just for tonight."

Next, Layla turned her attention to convincing Mikhail that an outing was a good idea.

Luckily, in that regard, Fred hadn't done anything to clue Mikhail in on Layla's plea for help. As far as the Semenov brothers knew, Layla was being nothing but cooperative. At least, that's what Layla thought. She hadn't heard from Ivan. Or Trent. Or Tabby, but that was another matter entirely.

In her gut, Layla felt like this part of her family's ordeal would be over and done with soon. It couldn't go on forever. Mikhail hadn't even brought an overnight bag with him. That led her to believe he hadn't intended to stay long.

She chuckled to herself as she thought about spy movies. Like Mikhail, the spies in the movies never seemed to carry much luggage.

"What's so funny?" Mikhail asked.

His tone wasn't hostile. Just curious. She couldn't mention spy movies with the girls around.

"Oh, nothing," she replied.

He wasn't going to take that for an answer. "Tell me. I want to laugh, too."

Layla bit her lip as she worked to come up with an answer that would satisfy everyone. "I was remembering our conversation from yesterday about the cookies and wondering if you'd seem out of place to the locals around here."

"Cookies?" Bethany asked.

Layla brushed her off with the wave of a hand. "It was a joke about how people call it tossing your cookies when you get sick and throw up. Mikhail found it funny."

She winked at him, and he smiled. He was growing more used to the kids and how to act around them. There was an ease that had developed.

With the mood effectively smoothed over, Layla went for it.

"So, Mikhail, will you join us at the Brick House Cafe for dinner? I know two little girls who are eager to get out of the house for a while. I don't see any harm."

He narrowed his eyes, turning the idea over in his mind. Raising one hand, he brushed his fingers lightly over the stubble that had grown on the sides of his head.

Once he'd made his decision, Mikhail stared hard at Layla as if to communicate what would happen if she tried anything that would go against the ground rules he'd established. She knew what he meant. She remembered what he'd said about her and the girls being an insurance policy to be sure Trent cooperated.

Layla nodded her agreement to remain under Mikhail's control. For now.

"Okay," he said, standing. He almost sounded excited about the idea. "We go. Everyone, get dressed in whatever you want to wear to this Brick House. Then we meet here at the front door. The dog must stay."

Hailey and Bethany cheered, then they laughed at the comment about Romeo.

"Romeo always stays home," Hailey added. "They don't allow dogs inside the restaurant. We could sit with him on the patio, but I like inside better. I like to look out the big windows into the courtyard next door. I watch the pigeons."

"Couldn't you do that from the patio?" Mikhail asked.

"I like to watch them through the window," Hailey replied with a gentle shrug.

Mikhail smiled and told the girl he understood. He didn't, necessarily, but he was being nice.

When their clothes were changed and they'd fancied themselves up, they all met at the front door as planned.

Since it might be dark by the time they'd return home, Layla closed the blinds and curtains, then turned on the porch light. She guided Romeo to his bed in the utility room. When all of the preparations were finished, the unusual foursome made their way to the Grant family's blue minivan in the garage. Layla helped Bethany into her booster seat and fastened her seatbelt, then climbed into the driver's seat and started the engine as Mikhail and Hailey got settled.

"All set?" she asked before placing the van in reverse.

"All set!" Hailey and Bethany replied in unison.

"Ready," Mikhail said.

As she backed out of the garage and maneuvered

around to exit the driveway facing forward, Layla surveyed the house that had been her family's happy home all these years.

She wasn't sure what would happen next.

She wasn't sure they'd ever return.

12

THE PUBLIC

"Table for four?" the young female hostess at the front desk asked.

Layla nodded. She wasn't sure how to act around Mikhail while under the observant eyes of the public.

Trent usually took the lead with things like driving, ordering, holding doors, and paying bills when they were out together. It had been a deliberate decision when they'd married to act in such a way that allowed them to look as normal as possible. They didn't want to stand out.

Layla wondered if she should defer to Mikhail now.

"Yes," Mikhail said, solving the problem. "Two kids."

"Follow me," the hostess said as she counted out two laminated adult menus and two paper kids' ones.

Layla was relieved that Mikhail had decided to speak up. She shot him a quick glance and an appreciative smile.

The young woman sat them at a table near the window that overlooked the courtyard. Hailey's preferred spot. "You can see the pigeons from here," she said to Mikhail as she climbed into the booth and motioned for him to sit down beside her.

"Good," he replied. "Can I sit here, by you?"

She nodded, and Mikhail sat down.

Bethany climbed into the booth opposite her sister, then Layla sat down in the last remaining seat. The girls leaned forward toward each other and began selecting crayons that suited their coloring needs.

"Meatloaf is on special," the hostess said. "Soup of the day is broccoli cheddar. Benton will be your server. He'll be here shortly. Enjoy!"

Mikhail thanked her. She said the same, then returned to her station near the door.

By the time Benton the server arrived, Layla was beginning to relax. She'd scanned the patrons and hadn't noticed anyone she knew. That was a good start. The less explaining she had to do, the better.

"Hey, I know you," Benton said before anything else.

Damn, Layla thought. She didn't recognize him. Maybe he had them confused with someone else.

"You do?" she asked.

The young man tapped his pen against his chin as if it would help solidify the memory. "Yeah," he said, nodding toward Mikhail. "I delivered groceries to your house the other day."

Mikhail stared blankly. Maybe he was unsure what to do.

"Harmon's Grocery," Benton clarified, lowering his voice and leaning lower near the table. "I work there delivering groceries during the day, and here in the evening. I'm sure I remember you, sir. You have one of those faces that's hard to forget."

"Is that so?" Mikhail asked. He shifted nervously in his seat.

Mikhail didn't strike Layla as the kind of man who would get nervous, but perhaps this scene was overwhelming him. It must be uncomfortable to look the part of a family man when you aren't the real deal. Especially given what he'd told her about having loved and lost a woman once.

"Yeah, I remember," Benton continued. "Big white house on the outskirts of town, long driveway, and a barking hound dog who sounded the alarm when I rang the doorbell. I thought he was going to bark his head off. He's loud, that one."

Hailey and Bethany glanced up at Benton a few times, but stayed focused on their coloring. They were listening in the way kids often do-- with only partial attention, yet ears wide open if something piqued their interest.

Mikhail nodded.

"You're Mr. Grant," Benton said matter-of-factly.

Layla and the girls opened their eyes wide, unable to keep their faces from showing the offense they felt at hearing Mikhail be mistaken for Trent.

No one at the table responded, but Benton filled the air time.

"I have a near photographic memory," he said as he leaned back on his heels in a proud stance. "I remember all the names and addresses I deliver groceries to. I can't help it. Couldn't if I tried. My boss at Harmon's appreciates my attention to detail though. Ms. Candler is a really nice lady. It's a shame what happened to the store last year… with the fire. I assume you heard?"

Finally, something Layla could latch onto. "Oh, I did hear about that. I'm so sorry."

Mikhail flashed her a glance, remembering their conversation about saying sorry. He didn't speak.

"Thank you," Benton said. "It wasn't a total loss. Not like they initially thought. Ms. Candler was able to salvage more than expected. She worked really hard to get the place rehabbed and back open. Now, here we are!"

He made a wide open gesture with his hands, almost like he was making a theatrical move in a Broadway play.

The young man seemed late high school or early college age. Perhaps Benton was a theater student. His symmetrical features, dark skin, and strong bone structure would certainly make him look appealing on stage.

"I'm glad to hear that," Layla replied.

Benton was personable, but didn't seem to know when to stop. "Harmon's has been around for so long," he continued. "Did you know that Ms. Candler's father, Clint Harmon, and her grandfather, Gus Harmon, were the original owners? Gus opened the doors all the way back in 1959. Ever since, that little store has stayed full. Folks around here love the place."

Layla nodded politely, but Mikhail was growing impatient. "Would you bring us some drinks?" he asked.

"Yeah, sure," Benton replied without skipping a beat. "What can I get you?"

Layla breathed a sigh of relief. Maybe they could get through dinner without having to say whether Mikhail was or was not Mr. Grant.

"Girls?" Mikhail asked. "Milk?"

They nodded sweetly. "Yes, Micky-Hail," Bethany said. "White milk. From the cows."

Benton tilted his head at the Micky-Hail reference, but managed to keep his chatter to a minimum. "And for Mom and Dad?" he asked.

Layla's skin crawled, the situation was so awkward.

"What do you have on tap?" Mikhail asked.

"Nothing," Benton replied. "But I can get you an adult beverage from the cooler. Bottled."

Mikhail grunted, then looked at Layla for a recommendation. She didn't have one. She wasn't much of a drinker. Eager to play the part and move this exchange along, though, she offered a suggestion.

"There's a craft brewery near here that makes a hard cider called Farmer's Red," Layla tried. "Might be worth a try. Unless you'd prefer one of Rosemary Run's famous local wines."

"We don't serve wine here," Benton added. "But we do have bottles of Farmer's Red."

Layla knew that. It had been something to say.

"Bring me a Farmer's Red," Mikhail confirmed. "And one for the lady."

"Oh, I don't drink. Not often, anyway," she explained while looking at Benton. She definitely did not want him to bring her the hard cider. Since she didn't drink often, she was more sensitive to the effects of alcohol than most people. She needed to keep her wits about her tonight. She couldn't let herself become inebriated.

"Nonsense," Mikhail said without looking at Layla. Then to Benton, "bring two."

"Coming right up," Benton said.

He scurried back to the kitchen to get things started.

Layla's face grew hot as she thought about how she'd handle herself if forced to drink the alcoholic beverage. She wasn't coming up with any good answers. For the millionth time since Mikhail had arrived, she wished she could go back to her normal life. Or even a new normal, for that matter. Surely, this wasn't it.

"Why did you do that?" she asked Mikhail.

The girls continued to color, unphased.

"What?" he replied. "You wanted to go out to dinner. Now we're out to dinner. Are you not happy to be here?"

"Of course, yes," she said. "I'm happy to be here."

"Then try to enjoy yourself."

Layla shook her head. As she did, she inadvertently made eye contact with a familiar woman on the other side of the dining room.

It was Bea Earl. Layla had met Bea when the girls had taken an art class she taught last winter. Bea was dining with what appeared to be her husband and son. When she saw Layla, a look of recognition immediately washed over her face. She smiled, then waved.

"Oh, no," Layla muttered.

"What's wrong now?" Mikhail asked.

"It's someone I know. Don't look now. She's…"

Before Layla could finish her sentence, Benton was back with their drinks.

"Two white milks and two Farmer's Reds," he said as he placed the beverages down on square napkins.

"Thank you," Mikhail said with an appreciative smile.

He took a swig of his Farmer's Red and smiled even bigger. "Very good," he confirmed.

Benton paused as if he wanted to launch into another story, but he held himself back. "What can I get you for dinner?" he asked.

Layla's face burned even hotter.

She felt herself growing angry at the progression of events that had left her here with a Russian hitman who was essentially holding her and the girls hostage, a chatty waiter who just so happened to have delivered groceries to the man he believed to be Mr. Grant, an alcoholic drink she'd be expected to down even though she didn't want to, and an impending and-- no doubt-- tense conversation with her children's art teacher about why they were dining with a stranger.

She hadn't even looked at the dinner menu.

Mikhail ordered a rare steak with a side of green beans and potatoes. *Figures*, Layla thought. The girls ordered chicken nuggets and grilled cheese, having agreed to split their entrees in half and share them. They were such good girls. So adaptable, and resilient.

"And for you?" Benton asked, turning his gaze to Layla.

She remembered what the hostess had said. The meatloaf was on special.

"I'll have the meatloaf," Layla said, foregoing her usual order of a grilled chicken salad in favor of something that would help minimize the effects of the alcohol.

"And for your sides?" Benton asked. "You get two."

Layla couldn't choose sides. All she could think about

was Bea's gaze on her. It was obvious that the woman was waiting for Benton to leave, then she'd make her way over to say hello.

"I don't know," Layla replied. "What's good?"

She immediately regretted asking Benton an open ended question.

"Oh, well, everything is good," he said. "But if you're asking what I like, I'd have to say the macaroni and cheese. It's to die for. The roasted asparagus isn't bad either. Same for the okra, and even the applesauce is solid. Does any of that sound appetizing this evening?"

Layla answered quickly. "I'll try the mac and the asparagus. Easy on the oil, please."

"The olive oil?"

She nodded.

"We don't use olive oil on our asparagus," Benton explained. "Sometimes, I wish we would. But here, we make a glaze with balsamic vinegar, lemon, and red pepper. You'll see. I expect you'll like it. Most people do…"

"Okay," she said. "I'm sure I will. Thank you."

Mikhail gave Benton an official-looking nod as a prompt to leave the table. The young man took the hint and returned to the kitchen once more to enter their entree orders into the computer system.

"He's a talker," Mikhail commented. "Nice boy, but busy at the mouth."

"Umm hmm," Layla said, distracted by Bea.

Bea was saying something to her husband while looking at Layla. It appeared that Bea was ready to stand and walk over.

"What were you about to say?" Mikhail asked. "About someone you know?"

Layla glanced in Bea's direction, and Mikhail turned to follow her gaze.

"Yes," she replied. "The girls' art teacher."

Hailey and Bethany snapped their heads around excitedly. They were big fans of their teacher, having thoroughly enjoyed her class. It's what had prompted the Grant family to convert the exercise room into an art studio.

"Mrs. Earl?" Hailey asked. "She's here?"

"Mrs. Earl! Mrs. Earl!" Bethany chanted while making paintbrush movements in the air with her little hands.

"That's right," Layla said reluctantly. "And oh, look. She's coming over to say hello."

IT'S COMPLICATED

Bea looked happy. The kind of happy that can only come from being in the proper flow with life and the Universe itself. She'd recently divorced her controlling ex-husband and married a new love, Travis, who seemed precisely right for her. Everything in her world had shifted in a positive direction once she'd decided to face up to old skeletons and make a change.

Layla knew Bea's story because the two women had become friends. Sort of. They weren't close friends like Layla and Tabby were, but they'd gone for lunch or tea together a number of times while the kids were in school.

Bea's schedule was usually flexible during school hours. Since Layla didn't work outside of the home, they were easily able to find time to get together. They hadn't seen each other all summer, though.

Layla wasn't sure if Bea had heard about Trent's legal troubles. She hoped not. At a minimum, Layla hoped for the chance to tell the story herself. Things often became twisted once the rumor mill got a hold of them.

"Layla, my friend, how are you? It feels like it's been ages since we've seen each other," Bea said as she approached the table.

Travis had stayed put at their table across the restaurant along with Bea's teenage son, Max.

"Bea, how great to see you," Layla replied.

She stood and the women kissed each other on the cheeks, Southern European style. Mikhail looked on, but didn't say anything. With that greeting out of the way, Bea turned to the girls.

"How are the beautiful and talented Grant girls?" she asked cheerfully. "Enjoying your summer?"

Hailey and Bethany lit up like little Christmas trees under Bea's attention. They talked a mile a minute, showing her their coloring on the restaurant's paper kids menus, recounting what they'd done all summer up until now, and pointing out the pigeons in the courtyard that could be seen through the large glass window beside them. Bea oohed and aahed at everything the girls told her.

When it came time to introduce Mikhail, the entire group fell into an awkward silence. Finally, Bea spoke.

"Hi, I'm Bea Earl," she said as she extended her hand toward him for a friendly shake.

"Mikhail Semenov," he replied, surprising Layla by giving his real name.

They hadn't talked about what name he'd use if he met anyone, but Layla didn't expect him to use his real one. Not his real last name, anyway. It sounded very Russian, which made the connection to her own past a little too close for comfort. It would be more difficult to say he was a cousin now. Couldn't he have said he was a Grant?

"Pleased to meet you, Mr. Semenov," Bea said politely.

"You can call me Mikhail," he replied. "And I'm pleased to meet you, too."

Bethany jumped in, unable to hold herself back. "Micky-Hail is staying at our house with us while Daddy is on a work trip."

Hailey shot her sister a look of warning, but it was too late. The damage had been done.

Layla blushed, her face turning as red as the leather on the seat below her. She didn't think the situation could be any more uncomfortable.

"Is that so?" Bea asked, unsure what to say in reply.

"Daddy has been gone for four days now," Bethany continued, holding up four fingers for emphasis. "We aren't allowed to go outside but we wanted to eat at a restaurant so Micky-Hail finally said okay."

"Okay, I think she gets the idea," Layla said nervously as she put an arm around Bethany and pulled her close.

"What Mama?" Bethany asked. "I'm pretending that Micky-Hail is your cousin. Like you said."

Layla closed her eyes and froze. She suddenly wanted to hide her head in the sand like an ostrich. She'd never understood the odd birds until now, but she instantly thought the creature could be her spirit animal.

Bea lowered her brow and glanced back at her husband and son. She didn't make eye contact with Mikhail. "Layla, is everything okay here?" she asked, her tone concerned.

"Sure thing," Layla said, putting on her best fake smile

and positive attitude. "Mikhail is an old childhood friend who is in town for a few days. It's been good to have him around."

Please don't ask where we're from, Layla thought to herself. *Please. Please. Please.*

"Umm hmm," Bea muttered. "Trent doesn't usually travel for work? Does he?"

She crossed her arms over her chest and tensed her shoulders. Bea was on guard, her suspicions raised, and they all knew it. Even Travis noticed from across the room. He sat up straighter in his seat and looked like he was considering getting up to come join his wife.

"Not usually," Layla said. "There's just a lot going on right now. Some high-level decisions have to be made. Trent is out conversing with colleagues about some upcoming changes."

Layla had learned long ago that it was best to tell partial truths when forced to omit information or to outright lie. The body was less likely to contradict your words that way. She'd done it plenty of times before when establishing her new American identity as Layla Grant, but she despised having to do it now, in front of the children. She felt trapped, backed into a corner like a wild animal who just wanted to be free.

"At the bank?" Bea asked.

This was getting to be too much. Mikhail gave Layla a look that said to get rid of her friend, or he would.

Realizing the seriousness of the matter, Layla had to think fast. She didn't want to leave the girls alone with Mikhail, but given the options, decided she had to. After all, she still didn't think he'd harm them. She needed to speak with Bea in private before this train went completely off the tracks.

"Bea, could I speak to you in private?" Layla asked.

Mikhail nodded slowly and half winked, letting her know that he approved of the move. The girls went back to their coloring. All seemed well for Layla to step away for a few minutes.

Bea hesitated, glancing back at Travis and Max again, but finally agreed. "Sure," she said.

"Good," Layla replied. "I was about to head to the ladies room, anyway. Care to join me?"

"Okay," Bea said. "After you."

Layla told the girls she'd be right back and to stay seated with Mikhail. They agreed, so Layla and Bea headed for the restroom.

They had to cross the entire dining room, zigging and zagging around partitions and between rows of tables. When they finally entered the restroom and the door closed behind them, Bea dropped all pretense at politeness and got right down to the matter at hand.

"What in the hell is going on?" Bea asked. "Are you and the girls in trouble?"

There was a lounge area in the front of the women's restroom that was large enough for a small sofa and a side table opposite a row of mirrors. Layla sat gingerly on one end of the sofa and leaned forward with her elbows on her knees. She felt like she might pass out.

"No, nothing like that," Layla lied.

"I'm sorry, but I'm not sure I believe you," Bea replied. "I was a woman with a secret who was then criticized and belittled by my husband for years. Believe me, I know the look of trouble on another woman's face when I see it."

Layla was trapped. There were no good answers. No good moves to get out of this unscathed. It was all about damage control now. She knew that Mikhail wanted her to appease Bea and find a way to get her off their backs. But Layla knew that her friend spoke the truth about recognizing trouble as a result of her own history. She took a deep, cleansing breath and prepared to tell the true story that word embarrass her while keeping the larger threat at bay.

"Okay, look," Layla said. "There is something going on. I didn't want to tell you because I'm ashamed. I've been trying to act like nothing is wrong, but it's exhausting to hold it all in."

"Go on," Bea said, her gaze so intense Layla thought it might burn right through her skin.

"You have to promise me you won't tell anyone what I'm about to share," Layla continued.

"Not even Travis?"

"Well, I guess you can tell him. But I don't want the word spreading around town. That will happen on its own soon enough," Layla explained.

Bea nodded, then walked into the back portion of the restroom to make sure no one was within ear shot. When she determined it was clear, she returned and sat beside Layla on the sofa.

"Okay," Bea said. "I promise you I know what this feels like. You can trust me." She grabbed Layla's hand and gave it a gentle squeeze. "It will feel good to get whatever this is off of your chest."

Layla nodded, then took another big, deep breath. She had to keep breathing, or else her lungs might fail her. Her body was running on some sort of weird emergency operating procedures. She couldn't explain it, but she felt all discombobulated, like some critical internal wiring was crossed.

She'd thought she'd known stress and tension during her early days as a sleeper agent in America. As it turned out, that was nothing compared to knowing that her husband and children were in danger.

"It's Trent," Layla said softly. "He's in trouble with the law and is being tried for bank fraud. He's scheduled to stand trial by jury next week."

Bea's eyes widened. Apparently, she hadn't heard. Layla thought that much was good.

"Are you serious?" Bea asked. "Next week?"

Layla nodded. She was speaking the truth. Hopefully, this truth was so shocking and awful that she wouldn't have to go into the even more shocking part. This should be enough for Bea to chew on. Enough to justify the unusual circumstances.

"Yes. We've know for a while that this was coming. Federal investigators raided our house a while back. Luckily, we live far enough out of town and away from prying eyes that no one noticed. Word will get out soon, though, whether I like it or not."

"Because of the trial?" Bea asked.

"That and the fact that Trent's colleague, Moe Griffith, is named as a co-conspirator," Layla continued.

"The former NFL football player? That Moe Griffith?"

"That's the one," Layla said.

Bea leaned back against the sofa as she processed the information. It was a lot to take in. Her eyes darted around the room as she thought about it all. Layla could see the moment she thought about what this would mean for the girls. Bea's face crumpled into a genuinely sad expression.

"Do you think they'll convict him?" Bea asked.

"I honestly don't know," Layla said as she raked a hand through her hair. It was all she could do to keep from breaking down into tears. "My nerves have been shot. Like I said, I'm embarrassed. Mortified, to be precise. But mostly, I don't want Trent to go away. I can hardly fathom what that will do to our sweet girls. They're so young. Babies, almost."

"Oh, Layla," Bea said. "I hate to hear all of this. Is there anything I can do? I could distract the girls with some art lessons. Maybe take them to the art museum in Sacramento for a day?"

"That's very kind of you," Layla replied. "Right now, I'm taking it one day at a time and keeping the girls close. I feel like we need to get a solid handle on what we're dealing with before I can make any solid plans, you know?"

Bea nodded. "Yeah, I get it."

They sat in silence for a few minutes while an older lady came in to use the bathroom and then made her exit. When she was gone, Bea scooted close to Layla and put an arm around her shoulders.

"Your secret is safe with me, Layla. I promise you," she said.

"Thank you," Layla replied, genuinely grateful. "As you could probably guess, we've just scratched the surface of my troubles."

"I guessed that, for sure," Bea confirmed. "I'm trying not to bombard you with questions, so I'll leave it to just one more, if that's okay with you."

Layla nodded. "Go ahead." She knew exactly what Bea would ask.

"Mikhail. Is he a good addition to your life? Or should I be worried about his presence?"

Layla chewed her lip as she decided how to respond. All she could come up with was, "it's complicated."

14

———

OUT OF PLACE

B y the time Layla and Bea finished their chat in the ladies' room, they had become famished. Both women were waiting for dinner to be served and were ready to eat. Agreeing that they'd catch up further in the coming days, they powdered their noses, freshened up their lipstick and opened the door to rejoin the crowd in the main dining area.

When the door opened, Layla's eyes landed on Hailey and Bethany. Thankfully, they were still at the table with Mikhail, coloring away and looking content.

Thank God, Layla thought.

She'd figured they'd be okay, but seeing that for herself was quite a relief.

"I'll stop by your table to say goodbye before we leave," Bea whispered as they prepared to part ways. "And we'll get together before next week. Right?"

"Sounds good," Layla replied. "Thanks again. I enjoyed our talk."

She had enjoyed the talk. Confiding in someone had

been cathartic. Maybe it wasn't so bad if people knew about Trent's legal issues. Maybe Layla needed the support of friends. Of course, all the friends Layla had would be shocked and outraged to learn the true nature of her background and business in the United States. But that was a problem for another day. Right now, her focus was on dealing with the Mikhail situation and looking for a way out.

Bea could be a comfort and a shoulder to cry on, but she wasn't the person who would help Layla and the girls get to safety. Not right now, anyway. The interaction between them this evening had been too public. It had already drawn too much attention. Layla needed someone less conspicuous. Like Fred.

She thought about the attorney again and hoped he was making some progress on suitable arrangements for her intent to pledge allegiance to the American government. She wondered how he would get in touch with her when he did have news to share.

For now, though, Layla pushed all of that out of her mind in favor of focusing on the meatloaf that would arrive at her table any moment now, steaming hot and flavorful. She returned to her seat and gave Mikhail a slow nod to let him know she had placated Bea.

"Have a good chat?" he asked as Layla got settled and spread her napkin over her lap.

Out of the corner of her eye, she noticed Travis turning to look at them again. Bea motioned for him to keep facing his own table. He did as she asked.

"Yes," Layla said. "I told her about our... *schedule* for next week, if you know what I mean." She eyed Mikhail knowingly as she said it. "That was enough to satisfy her curiosity. For now."

Layla hadn't specifically told Mikhail that the girls were in the dark about Trent's legal troubles, but he had gotten that idea. He didn't pry. The more time he spent with Layla and the girls, the more he came to understand that Layla had her ways. He could tell that Hailey and Bethany were good kids. He'd decided not to intervene in what was obviously working quite well. Although, he did wonder when Layla planned to tell them that their father was likely going to prison. They would have to find out, eventually. And if Trent wasn't going to prison, he might be going to Russia instead. Mikhail wasn't sure which would be the better outcome.

"I see," he said simply.

"I told you I could handle myself," Layla added. "You don't have to watch over me so closely."

Mikhail raised a hand to his jaw, leaning an elbow on the table top. "Really, now? Because Ivan..."

Layla stopped him before he could finish his sentence. "No talk of Ivan. Please."

Inevitably, Hailey felt compelled to inquire. "Who is Ivan?" she asked.

Layla shot Mikhail a dirty look before answering her daughter. "He's Mikhail's brother," she replied truthfully. "Now drink your milk. Dinner should be here any minute."

"Micky-Hail has a brother?" Bethany asked in her sweet little voice.

Layla nodded reluctantly. She didn't really want to get into all of this. She was weary from everything that had happened and just wanted to fill her belly. The hard cider still sat in front of her, waiting to be consumed. Meatloaf had to go first.

"Is he a big brother or a little brother?" Hailey tried. Now that the subject was being discussed, she wanted more details, too. Both of the girls were curious little people, curiosity being a hallmark of their developmental stage. They couldn't help themselves.

Before Mikhail could answer, Benton arrived with a large serving tray on his shoulder and a metal stand slung over one forearm. "Dinner's here!" he exclaimed as he propped the stand up and set the tray down on top of it. The whole maneuver looked precarious, but he made it work.

"Good thing," Layla said. "I'm starving."

"Okay, little ladies first," Benton said as he set a pair of bright blue plates down in front of the girls. "Be careful. It's hot."

"Thank you!" they chirped in unison.

Benton pulled a black cloth napkin from his apron and made a big show out of picking up Layla's larger plate from the tray. It was apparently even hotter the the girls' had been. Steam rose from the food and smelled scrumptious.

"I guess I shouldn't say big ladies next, should I?" the young man quipped, clearly amused by himself. He threw his head back and laughed.

"Probably not a good idea," Mikhail said dryly.

"Mature ladies next?" Benton tried, pausing dramatically with Layla's dinner plate on his outstretched hand.

She hesitated, not in the mood for the young man's antics. Benton seemed like he wanted to wait but soon lowered the plate to the table, unable to hold it any longer.

"Thank you," Layla said.

Benton served Mikhail without fanfare. Perhaps he was finally getting the idea that they weren't in the mood to chat.

"Okay, then," he said, resting his hands on his hips as he surveyed the table. "Can I get you anything else right now?"

Mikhail looked over the table as well. "How about some more milk for the girls? And another Farmer's Red for me? It's tasty."

Benton nodded. "Coming right up. Enjoy!"

As he placed the tray under one arm and folded up the metal stand, Bea was suddenly there, waiting behind him. Benton excused himself and returned to the kitchen.

"Bea," Layla said. "Our food just arrived…"

"I know it did. I'm sorry," she said. "There's something that needs your attention. Please, come with me."

Layla stared at her friend, perplexed. She was so hungry. She certainly didn't want to get up and leave the table while her food got cold. She wasn't even sure Mikhail would be willing to wait on her to eat when she returned. This was the first meal they'd shared together at a restaurant, after all.

"Can it wait a few minutes? I'd like to get some food in me."

Mikhail picked up his fork and knife and began to cut his steak. Taking his cue, Hailey and Bethany began to eat as well. They quickly divided their entrees so they'd each have both chicken nuggets and half of a grilled cheese sandwich, then they dug in, eating hungrily.

Layla craned her neck and looked around the restaurant to see if she might figure out what Bea was referring to. Only Bea put a hand out to stop her before she could survey the section of the restaurant closest to the restrooms, where they had already been.

"Bea, what has you stirred up?" Layla asked.

Mikhail didn't seem concerned. Layla thought maybe she shouldn't be either. But the look on her friend's face told her otherwise.

"Fine," she said, pushing her plate forward and tossing her napkin down on the table in front of her. "But make it quick, I beg you."

Mikhail nodded his approval, so Layla followed Bea back toward the restroom, through the rows of tables and around the partitions. The place was growing more crowded as peak dinner time came into full swing. Layla assumed they were going back to the small sofa in the ladies' room, but Bea stopped her just short of the door.

Crouching behind a partition that was topped with green plants, Bea pulled Layla's hand, moving them both down low and out of sight.

"What are we doing here?" Layla asked.

"Shh," Bea replied. "Whisper."

Layla's eyes grew big with emphasis. "What are we doing here?" she asked again, much quieter this time.

"I hate to be the bearer of bad news-- I really do-- but there's something you need to see."

Layla's pulse quickened at this news, but she couldn't

imagine what it was. How could anything she'd see be worse than what she was already going through. It didn't seem possible. The girls were safe back at their table, and Layla was making it through Mikhail's stay, hour by hour and day by day.

"What is it?"

It was Bea's turn to close her eyes for a beat and collect herself.

"Now you're scaring me," Layla said. "Just tell me."

"Okay," Bea said, the sadness evident in her voice. "Over there, tucked in that corner booth."

Bea raised her head high enough above the partition to point. Layla matched Bea's stance and followed her gaze. Almost immediately, she saw it. The sight nearly broke her heart into pieces.

"Oh, my God," Layla said. "What in the hell?"

Her mouth moved, but the rest of her remained frozen in place, trying desperately to process what she was witnessing.

There, in the corner booth, was Trent. He was smiling, laughing, and leaning close to none other than Layla's supposed best friend, Tabby Rhodes. The two were huddled together, wine glasses half empty and dinner half eaten. The other side of the booth was empty, suggesting that they had chosen to sit close together.

"There must be an explanation," Layla muttered. "I can't... I mean..."

"Did you say Trent was out of town?" Bea asked. Her tone was compassionate, not accusatory.

"I... I... yes, but..." Layla stammered.

Bea shook her head. "There's no need to be

embarrassed," she said. "You didn't do anything wrong here."

Layla whipped her head around to face Bea. "How do you know Trent did? Maybe there's a good reason…"

Bea sighed and shook her head again. "Keep watching. Travis noticed them come in, looking all lovey-dovey."

Layla turned back toward her husband and did as Bea suggested. For the better part of five minutes, they watched. Trent and Tabby cooed and leaned close, touching each other's hands, arms, and finally faces. At first, it seemed like the behavior could be dismissed as friendly. Socially acceptable, even. But the way they looked at each other and the way their touches lingered told another story.

"I can't watch," Layla said through tears.

"You have to," Bea said. "Believe me. I was cheated on. And unfortunately, at one point when Travis and I first got together, I was cheating, too. It's better to know the truth. To get everything out in the open." Layla shook her head, but Bea put a supportive hand on her back. "Watch."

No sooner did Layla wipe her eyes and refocus than it happened. Trent leaned in and kissed Tabby on the lips with an open mouth. His body stiffened, enjoying the sensation. Tabby's body responded, too, her back arching and her chest rising to meet him. They were on fire for each other. *Definitely* more than friends.

Layla tore away, running full speed out the front door as tears streamed down her face.

PART III

DEFECTS

15

WHEN YOU KNOW

For what felt like hours, Layla sat within the safety of her minivan in the parking lot. Bea had tried to accompany her, but Layla had begged to be left alone. It had taken some convincing, but Bea had finally agreed to return to her dinner inside the restaurant, leaving Layla to grieve alone.

At a time like this, Layla wished she had family to call on. Real family. The kind that had known you all your life and still loved and protected you anyway. She wished she could hug her own mama, her papa, and her siblings. She wished she'd never left her village and had never agreed to become a sleeper agent. Most of all, she wished she'd never fallen in love with Dmitriy Kozlov. She'd hinged her whole life around the belief that he would be loyal and true to her. How wrong she had been.

The betrayal stung. It left a bad taste in her mouth. The hurt went deep.

As she sat in the minivan watching happy couples and families file in and out of Brick House Cafe, Layla's emotions ricocheted from disbelief to denial, to anger, and everything in between. In all of the scenarios she'd ever imagined for her life and future, this had not been one of them. The fact that the other woman was her closest friend only made the deception that much worse.

Layla felt completely and utterly broken. She'd sobbed so hard that her shoulders hurt. There was no way to recover from the mortal wound she'd been dealt.

Not now. Not ever.

Yet Layla had to recover because the next trio to emerge from the cafe was her very own. Hailey and Bethany each held one of Mikhail's big hands. The girls carried plastic cups with colorful straws in their free hands, apparently milk to-go. They must not have spotted their father on the way out. They looked unphased. In fact, they looked happy, as if they'd had a good meal with Mikhail.

Remembering where they'd parked, Mikhail turned and made his way to the blue minivan. Seeing them coming, Layla flipped down the visor to check her face. It was a wreck. Her eyes were nearly swollen shut from all the crying. Her nose was red, and her mascara ran down her cheeks in heavy black streaks. She quickly pulled a paper napkin out of the glove compartment and did her best, fast fix-up job in the short time it took Mikhail and the girls to reach her. It barely made a difference. There would be no way to avoid them finding out that something was very wrong.

"Why did you come outside, Mama?" Hailey began, opening one of the sliding doors and climbing inside.

She didn't notice her mom's face at first, but stopped

in her tracks when she caught a glimpse in the rearview mirror. Bethany climbed into the other side, then immediately stopped to see what had her sister alarmed. She, too, caught a glimpse of her mother's face in the mirror and froze. Neither of them had ever seen Layla so upset.

Layla had never been so upset. Not even close.

"It's okay," Layla said as Mikhail closed the door behind Bethany and climbed into the passenger seat. "I'm okay."

"Whoa," Mikhail said. "What's happening?"

Layla looked at the three of them, their faces innocent and trusting, then she burst into another round of tears. She heaved and sobbed, her very spirit in the throes of deep distress. She didn't want to scare the girls, but she couldn't hold her emotions inside. She felt like she'd been gutted like a fish at the market, without care or compassion.

"S… s… sorry…" Layla stammered. "I'm…"

She could even finish her sentence.

"Is there someone I can call?" Mikhail asked.

Layla knew his offer was a big deal, especially considering his orders to keep an eye on her and the girls at all times. He was loosening the reins, a lot.

She shook her head, and sobbed harder. The two people Layla would have called were actively betraying her, right now, as they spoke. How unfair and cruel to find herself in this situation.

"Mama, you're scaring Bethany," Hailey said softly.

Her little voice was tentative. She was afraid, too, but

she was looking out for her little sister. It was all too much for Layla to handle.

"I'm sorry," Layla managed. "I'm okay."

Mikhail turned his head around to make eye contact with the girls in the back seat. He took one look at them, and sprang into action. Deliberately and without hesitation, he exited through the passenger door, then walked around to the driver's side of the van. He opened the door gently as Layla continued to heave and sob, her breathing short and fitful.

"Come on," he said gently. "I'll drive us back to the house."

Layla shook her head and opened her mouth to object, but another wave of sadness overtook her and she closed her eyes tightly. She couldn't speak.

Mikhail reached out his hand for hers, which she took. He helped her stand, then placed an arm around her shoulders as he walked her to the passenger seat and helped her sit down. She was trembling.

Before Mikhail closed the door, he leaned close to Layla's ear and whispered, "Petra is a strong woman. She will be alright."

Layla nodded her appreciation, then closed her eyes and let Mikhail take care of her. It was strange and good, all at the same time. She was grateful that he was there-- especially for the girls.

The ride home was uneventful. Everyone stayed silent in the van. Layla and the girls looked out the windows as if it was the thing to do, even though they could see very little in the low light of the setting sun. Purples, pinks, and oranges had streaked the blue sky, but those colors had faded into blackness now. There was a full moon on the rise. It looked ready to illuminate the sky soon enough.

Layla thought there was probably a metaphor for life in there somewhere, but she was too weary to find it.

Mikhail drove them slowly and carefully, and Layla was surprised by his tenderness. She thought maybe they could be friends. After all, he was certainly acting like a friend right now. The only real friend she had, when you got right down to it.

Bea was a nice person, but she and Layla didn't have the proper chemistry to become close friends. Not yet, anyway. Besides, Layla had completely misjudged Tabby. She thought maybe she'd be better off to keep male friends rather than female ones. It sounded reasonable, but Layla knew she shouldn't make any big decisions one way or another. She was too out of sorts, thanks to the emotional blow she'd received.

When they arrived home and pulled into the driveway leading to the Grant family's big white house, an unusual station wagon was parked near the front walkway, just before the carriage house and garage.

"Were you expecting a visitor?" Mikhail asked.

His tone was serious, but still kind. He wasn't accusing.

Layla shook her head. "No, I wasn't. I don't recognize the car."

Upon more careful inspection, the wagon was a restored Mercedes-Benz. Layla was no expert when it came to old cars, but she suspected the vehicle was an early eighties model. It was blue. The color of a robin's egg. The owner clearly took excellent care of the car. It was immaculate.

"Wait here," Mikhail said as he got out of the van. "I'll check it out."

Layla and the girls all nodded. It was remarkable the way the four of them were functioning as a cohesive unit now, as if they'd been one all along. Mikhail made his way around the front of the house and onto the porch.

They could hear barking from inside the house. "Romeo," Hailey commented.

"He probably wants to go potty outside," Bethany added.

"We'll get him soon," Layla said. She was grateful to find words. She thought that just maybe, she had cried herself out for a little while. Maybe her body would give her a reprieve during which she could regain some strength.

They waited several minutes, then finally, Mikhail emerged from the front porch. He had Romeo under one arm, the dog's leash in hand.

"He didn't have a key, as far as I knew," Layla said.

Hailey jumped in to explain. "He has all of your keys, Mama. Your house key is on the ring with one that starts the van."

"Oh, yeah," Layla replied. "That's my smart girl."

Hailey smiled as she, her sister, and her mom continued to watch Mikhail approach the van. As he came closer, they could see a smaller, older man trailing behind him.

"Fred!" Layla exclaimed. She was mighty glad to see him.

Layla unbuckled and got out of the van to greet the old man. She hadn't met him in person before, but she'd seen a photo on his law firm's website. It had to be the same man. And if Mikhail looked this calm, he must be okay with her talking to him.

"Mrs. Grant?" Fred asked. He stepped close to her and extended his hand to shake.

"That's right," she replied, although being called by Trent's last name suddenly rubbed her the wrong way. She let it go.

"I'm Fred Lowell, your husband's defense attorney."

The girls had exited the van and were listening like little hawks.

"Mama, what's a defense attorney?" Bethany asked.

Then more directly, Hailey asked the man, "do you know my daddy?"

Layla and Mikhail glanced at each other. If she was going to speak with Fred, it would have to be in private. She wondered if Mikhail would allow it?

Thinking fast, Layla decided the back patio would be the best place. There were lights out there, along with a firepit and large pieces of outdoor furniture with soft cushions. Layla and Trent had designed the space for entertaining, but had done precious little of it. Layla thought it ironic that it would be used for a conversation with Fred that could potentially dismantle their entire lives. Yet, here she was at that juncture. She'd do what she must.

Fred smiled, avoiding the girls' questions. He looked at Layla, his expression serious. "Is there someplace private we could talk?"

Layla hesitated a moment, her senses dulled from exhaustion. She caught up soon enough, though. "Of course. Girls, go inside with Mikhail and wash up for bed. If you want, you can have a fruit popsicle first."

Upon hearing that, the girls cheered and made their way into the house, quickly forgetting about the questions they'd asked of Fred. Mikhail followed along behind them, stopping only briefly to give Layla a look of warning.

I know, I know, she thought as she looked back. "I'll be in soon," she said.

When the front door had closed and she and Fred were alone, she took him by the forearm. "Do you have news? About what we talked about."

He looked around, apparently to make sure no one was listening. "I do. Yes."

"Then let's get right to it," Layla said as she looped one arm through his and led him around back.

16

BURDEN OF PROOF

Layla had a grandpa once. Back in Russia, she'd been quite close to him as a child. *Dedushka.* The word tickled her mind as she thought it, though she dared not say it out loud.

"Watch your step," she said to Fred as they stepped over a section of landscaping and onto the cobblestone patio.

Fred was frail, whether he realized it or not. He was still actively practicing law, but years of long days and late nights had, apparently, taken their toll. He reminded Layla of her grandpa.

An image of herself as a little girl, eating cheese and crackers with her grandpa, flashed vivid in Layla's mind. Her grandpa had always liked a certain cheese spread made with carrots and garlic. *Syrnyi pashtet.*

When her grandpa knew little Layla was coming over, he'd make the spread and set out a plate of square crackers to go along with it. They'd eat the delicious snack together, often while sitting in the tiny kitchen of her grandparents' humble home, across from each other at the small table. In her mind's eye, she could still see the shadows the tall trees made outside. She could still smell the dampness of the woodsy setting mingling with the buttery smell of the cheese and crackers.

What Layla wouldn't give to go back. To see her dedushka again.

"A penny for your thoughts?" Fred asked as he settled onto a cushioned patio chair and crossed one leg at the knee.

Layla sat across from the old man, debating how much to tell him.

"Nothing much on my mind," she attempted to lie.

He wasn't buying it. Who would?

"Ma'am," Fred began. "No offense, but I've made a career out of knowing when people are telling the truth and when they have something to hide. Your face, while pretty, tells a very different story than your words do."

Layla sighed, tears stinging at her eyes again.

She didn't want to cry. Not in front of Fred.

"What has you so upset?" he tried.

She hated to share her family's personal business, but she knew it would be good to get this matter off her chest. And besides, there was attorney-client privilege to think about. Fred would be precluded from repeating anything she told him. Or so Layla thought.

"Do you promise to keep this between us?" she asked.

"If I'm to represent you, then there's…"

"Attorney-client privilege," they said at the same time.

"Right," Layla followed. "Okay, well, I just found out that my husband is having an affair. He's… *cheating* on me."

The words felt like acid coming out. Layla wished she could stuff them somewhere they wouldn't hurt her, but there was no such place. No such comfort.

"I'm sorry to hear that," Fred replied.

"Thanks," she said quickly. Layla wasn't very experienced at confiding in others. It was slow going. "To add insult to injury," she continued, "he's cheating with my best friend. I saw them kissing at dinner a while ago. At Brick House Cafe, for everyone to see. It was pathetic! The girls think she's their aunt, for God's sake." Then, "who knows? Maybe she'll end up being their stepmom."

"I'm sorry," Fred said again. "That sounds awful. Did your daughters see?"

"I don't think so. At least, there's that."

Layla leaned forward, resting her elbows on her knees. If she had been a smoker, she would have wanted a cigarette right now. She needed something to hold. Something to fidget with.

For the first time, she thought maybe she understood why addicts are so nervous and twitchy. They must have big, burdensome traumas they can't get away from. The substances they abuse seem to help. Layla figured when a person is in that much pain, maybe they should be allowed whatever coping mechanisms they like.

Fred stared at Layla, sizing her up. "You have a remarkable mastery of the English language for a foreigner. I'm impressed. You use slang phrases and idioms that non-natives tend to have trouble with. That may help your case. You'll seem more relatable."

Instinctively, Layla whipped her head around toward the back of the house, worried that the girls might have overheard. Luckily, they could be seen through the open windows. They were sitting at the dining room table with Mikhail. It looked like they were preparing to play a board game. And, no doubt, still excited about their fruit popsicles.

"They can't know," she said, gesturing toward the house.

Fred studied her further before he spoke. Then finally, "it's only a matter of time, Mrs. Grant."

"I know, but I intend to push it off as long as I possibly can. They're so little. They didn't ask for any of this. They shouldn't be punished and made to suffer for our-- *my*-- choices."

Layla silently cursed Trent, though she knew she had to focus on taking responsibility for her part. It was the only reasonable way to proceed. She was a grown woman. A mother, who had to protect her children above all else.

But damn that snake, she thought.

"Fair enough," Fred replied. "So, is it only your husband's infidelity that has your eyes all swollen and your nose all red? If I didn't know better, I'd think you'd been in a fight. Kind of seems like there's more to the story."

"There is," Layla confirmed hesitantly, brushing a clump of blonde hair from her eyes. "But it's complicated."

"Oh? Is romance in bloom between you and Mr. Mom in there?"

Layla was surprised by the question, even though she shouldn't have been. "What? No! Absolutely not. It isn't like that. We're just friends."

"Friends?" Fred pressed. "Isn't he the Russian handler sent to keep tabs on you and your children?"

Layla hesitated once more, unsure how to describe her relationship with Mikhail. She wasn't sure Mikhail would know how to describe it, if asked, either.

"Tell me I'm wrong," Fred added. His intense gaze bore deep into Layla, eyes like laser beams.

"You're not wrong," Layla said. "It's just that…"

"You're *friends* now," he said, finishing her sentence.

Fred didn't seem quite so grandfatherly when it felt like he was cross-examining Layla at trial. In fact, he seemed more and more evil all the time. He had a Jekyll-and-Hyde thing going on. Part nice old man and part savage beast who would turn on you without even a moment's notice.

"I guess we are friends, yes," she confirmed. "I don't think Mikhail is a bad guy. As it turns out, he's from the same small village I am. His father owns a pub in Russia that my family used to frequent. It's called Alexi's. Charming place."

"Those connections are nice, but the U.S. government will want to ensure your loyalty if they are to protect you. You do understand that, right? Any deal we can strike will depend on it."

Layla got excited at the mention of a possible deal. Her eyes came alive. "Have you asked them yet? Will they help me?"

Fred shifted his weight while maintaining eye contact with her. "I've made a few inquiries."

He didn't elaborate. Layla could hardly stand the suspense. "And?"

"And I need to know for absolutely certain what you want to do. Same for your husband. I'll need to speak with him."

"He still hasn't been in touch?" Layla asked.

"No, he hasn't, and we're running out of time. If you must know, I'm growing concerned that he won't be adequately prepared for his bank fraud case. Or worse, that he won't even show up to court. All of that is separate from any discussion of your ties to Russia. Your husband's situation is extremely complicated."

She scoffed, anger bubbling up inside. "I guess he's been too busy galavanting around town with his tongue down my best friend's throat. Or I guess I should say, my *former* best friend. Damn them both!"

Layla immediately regretted her outburst. It had come out of nowhere, like a switch had been flipped at the mention of Trent. Her so called *husband*.

What a waste of time, she thought.

She started to apologize, but didn't. In this instance, her anger was more than justified. Fred ought to understand that.

Crickets chirped as a long silence stretched between them, Fred tapping one toe in the air.

Layla stared at the patio stones formed in a circle beneath them. Trent had installed the stones himself. She could remember the day like it was yesterday.

She'd been pregnant with Hailey then, and she and Trent had been pinching pennies after buying the house. Layla had really wanted a nice space out back to entertain, but had been reluctant to spend the money. That Mother's Day, she'd awakened to the sounds of clanking and banging out back. She'd found Trent on his hands and knees, smoothing a sand and concrete mixture around the stones. He'd told her to consider it one of the many ways he intended to show his appreciation for her contributions as a wife and a mom.

To his credit, Trent had done just that, never taking Layla for granted, until now. Or so it had seemed. How could that have been the same man who would run off with Tabby? It didn't make sense.

"Thinking about your husband's betrayal?" Fred asked, his gaze unrelenting.

Layla turned her head to one side and raised a hand to cover her face. It was silly to think the pose would give her any real privacy, but she couldn't help trying.

Taking a cleansing breath, she gathered her thoughts and turned to face Fred. "Look," she began, "I can't speak for Trent. It seems he's gone mad. I don't know about him. What I do know is that I want protection for myself and my girls. I'll do anything to get it. I want to stay in America. This place is their home. The only one they've ever known. It would be traumatic for them if they were forced to go to Russia. Even worse if we had to be separated because I had to return to Russia."

"Is there someone they could stay with, should that happen?" Fred asked.

Layla shook her head. "No one except Tabby. And I don't see that happening."

Fred nodded. "You might not like it, but it's good to know that there is someone the girls could stay with. If it came to that."

Layla sputtered, choking back tears.

"Better than ending up in the foster care system," Fred added.

"I guess," she conceded.

The thought of being separated from Hailey and Bethany was unfathomable to Layla. She could hardly conceive of it.

Fred leaned forward, looking even more intense. "I hope I don't have to tell you the seriousness of your situation. Forget about your husband for a moment. Your personal situation is precarious. As I'm sure you know, Russia doesn't take it well when their agents betray them. It happens. Agents defect. But it's extremely difficult and it doesn't happen often."

"I know," Layla said. "It isn't like I'm a high-level operative or anything. I'm of little consequence in the grand scheme of things."

"I'm not sure the Russian government would see it that way," Fred said. "You hold information that could compromise them."

Layla shrugged. "Maybe."

One of Fred's eyes began to twitch. It immediately caught Layla's attention. At first, she wondered if it was a medical issue. Perhaps he was having a seizure or something. Upon further inspection, she decided it was probably some sort of nervous tic. A tell of some sort. She remained quiet to let him speak in the hopes of learning what had prompted the twitch.

Soon enough, Fred filled the air space. "I'm curious, Mrs. Grant. Do you feel any loyalty to your home country? I mean, you must have loved your parents once. Your siblings. Aunts, uncles, grandparents. If you hadn't, I suspect you wouldn't be a devoted mother like you clearly are now."

Layla considered the question. "Of course, I loved my family in Russia," she said.

"And do you feel loyalty to your home country?"

"That isn't a black and white question. It may sound like it to you. I know Americans are a patriotic bunch. I, too, now feel connected to the American people. I've spent fifteen years here, singing the national anthem at ballgames, raising my hand over my heart at the sight of the American flag, and feeling proud of those who volunteer to serve this country in the military. I've known people from Rosemary Run who have gone into the military and risked their lives for the American way of life that we hold dear."

"Really?" Fred asked.

"Yes, absolutely," Layla explained. She pointed to a section of woods facing the road. "A neighbor's boy enlisted in the U.S. Marine Corps last year. I watched him grow up. He used to mow our grass, when he was in high school. Now, he's stationed in the Middle East where things are volatile and dangerous."

"Is that so?"

Layla nodded. "Tommy Galliano, is his name. I looked into the kid's eyes. I saw the pride he has in America. I feel that pride, too."

Fred pursed his lips and ran a hand over his forehead. It was beginning to glisten in the humid night air. "Mrs. Grant, forgive me, but I notice that you didn't answer my question."

"I did."

"No, you didn't," he said. "I asked if you feel loyalty to your home country. You avoided answering, not once, but twice."

Layla threw her hands into the air, then thought better of it and gently placed them in her lap. "What do you want from me?"

"That's easy. I want you to want this. If you expect me to help you, I need to know that you genuinely care about becoming a real American citizen, and not just for your girls. Our government will need you to be sure."

"I am sure!" Layla exclaimed.

"Then you had better get busy coming to terms with what you're giving up."

17

THE PEACE

"Mikhail?" Layla said as they sat across from each other at the breakfast table.

It was day five since Trent's departure. It was day one since Layla had learned of her husband's betrayal.

"Yes?"

"I want to tell the girls."

Hailey and Bethany were still upstairs getting dressed for the day. Layla had called them for breakfast. They'd be down any minute.

"Tell them what?" Mikhail asked as he wolfed down a sausage link.

A big man like Mikhail had to eat a lot to keep his strength up.

"Everything," Layla confirmed.

Mikhail's eyes grew big. "Wait, weren't you shooting daggers at me with your eyes a few days ago when I said your real name?"

"Yeah, well, that was then and this is now. A lot has happened in a few days."

Mikhail tilted his head to one side and nodded as he chewed. "True," he said.

"Speaking of which," Layla continued, "what are we doing here? Now that I know Trent is with Tabby instead of Ivan, it doesn't make sense for you to stay."

She had told him about seeing Trent with Tabby at the restaurant after the girls had gone to bed last night.

Mikhail stopped chewing and looked in Layla's eyes. For a split second, she thought she recognized sadness on his face. She felt sad at the prospect of him leaving, too, but she was in a take-charge mood this morning. This houseguest situation couldn't go on forever.

He collected himself and resumed his tough-guy persona. "I wait until Ivan tells me it's time to leave," he said.

"And he hasn't done that yet?"

"No, he hasn't," Mikhail confirmed.

Layla stared at him, wondering how to broach the subject of them becoming friends. She wanted to come right out and ask if he might help her and the girls. She could use a friend on the inside to afford whatever protection possible from Russia. Maybe Mikhail knew someone who could convince those in charge to let her go without a fight.

"Why do you want to tell the little girls all of your heavy, adult problems?" he asked. "I see now. They're too young. Too innocent. If you tell them, it will change them."

"Like it changed us?" Layla said before thinking it through.

She hadn't spoken of such things before. She wasn't sure why she was bringing them up with Mikhail now.

"Anyway," Layla went on, "I'm not your prisoner anymore."

"You never were," Mikhail mumbled.

Layla leaned forward, hands splayed in front of her on the table. She hadn't made herself a plate of food yet.

"Well, you know what I mean. I'm not your insurance policy. Neither are those girls. You can stay here, but as our guest. Got that?"

Mikhail placed his fork and knife down on his empty plate and folded his arms across his chest. "Petra, what are you up to?" he asked, his brows low above his eyes. "You have my attention. You fiery woman, you."

Layla laughed. "I am righteously pissed off… about a lot of things. If that makes me fiery, then so be it."

Mikhail nodded. "Tell me more."

Before Layla could say more, the sounds of little footsteps rang out through the house as Hailey and Bethany praced down the stairs and made their way to the table. They were in good spirits this morning, apparently buoyed by last night's dinner at Brick House Cafe.

"Well, don't you seem happy," Layla said to her daughters. They each stopped to allow her a kiss on the cheek before they sat down and filled their plates.

"We are happy, Mama," Hailey said. "Last night was fun."

"It was fun," Mikhail said, smiling.

"Yeah!" Bethany agreed. "It was fun for me, too."

"Can we go out again tonight?" Hailey asked sweetly.

Layla smiled, too. There was a restaurant downtown called Honey Hog that Bea had been recommending for some time. Perhaps they could go there. Layla allowed herself to get excited at the prospect of another dinner out, as long as they didn't run into Trent and Tabby again.

Knowing about Trent's infidelity had freed Layla somehow. She loved her husband and was crushed by his betrayal, but Bea had been right. It was better to know. At least, that way, they could all move on. Layla could move on. She *needed* to move on. For her sake, and for the girls'.

"I don't know," Layla said. "Maybe. What do you think, Micky-Hail? There's a place I've been meaning to try. It's called Honey Hog."

The girls giggled at her use of Bethany's nickname for Mikhail.

"Yeah, Micky-Hail," Hailey said, joining in the fun. "Can we go to Honey Hog?"

"I'll tell you what," Layla said, before Mikhail had a chance to answer. "If Micky-Hail doesn't want to go, then he can stay here and the three of us will go alone."

The girls' faces grew long and their eyes wide upon hearing this. They also grew quiet. So quiet, you could have heard a pin drop. The only sound in the house at that moment was Romeo, who had lumbered in and plopped down at Mikhail's feet. The tags on his collar jingled as he settled.

"Would you look at that?" Layla said, gesturing to the dog. "He was scared of Micky-Hail a few days ago. Now it seems that they've become good buddies."

Hailey and Bethany remained quiet while they waited for Mikhail to show some sign that he would allow Layla's bold statements to stand. The girls couldn't articulate the subtleties of the situation, but they could feel the group dynamics shifting.

Mikhail leaned back in his chair, paused a moment, then stood and took his dirty plate to the sink. He stopped at the refrigerator on the way back. "Juice, girls?" he asked, holding a pitcher in anticipation of them saying yes.

"Yes, please," Bethany replied.

"Umm hmm," Hailey agreed.

He walked to the table slowly and poured the juice. When each girl had a full cup, he set the pitcher down on the table carefully. They all looked at each other, waiting for his response.

"Okay, okay," he said. "I'm in. Let's all go to Honey Hog tonight. Should I make a reservation?"

"Sure!" Layla said cheerfully. "Bea says it's kind of fancy, but in a rustic way. If that makes sense."

"Kind of like Alexi's," Mikhail replied.

"Kind of, yeah," Layla confirmed. "She told me lots of details about the place-- exposed wooden beams lining an arched ceiling, elegant pendant lights dangling down towards the reclaimed wood tables set with white cloth napkins, artisan dinnerware, and even crystal vases filled with sprigs of fresh-cut rosemary. New owners bought the place recently. Bea says they invested a pretty penny to renovate it from top to bottom."

"Can we wear dresses?" Hailey asked.

"If you want to," Layla replied.

"And lipstick?" Bethany tried.

The girls knew they were too young to wear lipstick other than clear gloss on special occasions.

Layla chucked and looked at Mikhail. "You know what? Sure. I don't see the harm in it. Lip gloss, though. Not lipstick."

The girls cheered in their usual, enthusiastic way.

"Okay, Mama!" Hailey said. "Thank you."

Layla and Mikhail looked at each other, and Layla thought about what to tell her daughters and when. Maybe Mikhail had been right about not burdening them with adult problems. She supposed that was especially true when it came to issues that were yet to be resolved. Things might look a lot different a year from now, a month from now, or even a week from now. Maybe it was better to wait. To know more before burdening them.

Layla and the girls turned their attention back to breakfast. They were piling food on their plates when the doorbell rang.

Mikhail stood. "I'll get it," he said. "I'm finished eating."

"Are you sure?" Layla asked. "It might be a nosy neighbor or grocery delivery person. If so, it might make things easier if we don't have to go through a lengthy explanation about who you are."

Mikhail shook his head as he walked toward the front door. "Sit. Eat. I'll be right back."

Layla listened as his heavy steps approached the door. Mikhail was dressed in his own clothes, freshly washed again, all except the leather jacket. He had already put on his boots. She heard him pause, presumably to look through the peephole or one of the living room windows. She couldn't get a full view of him from where she was sitting.

Romeo lifted his head and cocked it to one side to listen, but he didn't move from his place on the floor underneath the table.

"Who is it?" she called.

Mikhail didn't answer.

Layla heard the door fly open fast, then slam again. Then she heard Mikhail's footsteps on the front porch. They were quick, tactical. Before she had time to react, the door slammed again with Mikhail inside. He locked the deadbolt and chain, his fingers moving at lightning speed.

"Get down!" he yelled.

"What are you talking about?" Layla tried, confused by what was happening.

"Get down! Now!" Mikhail yelled again, just seconds before bullets began shattering the living room windows.

"Oh, my God," Layla muttered as she dove for the girls. They shrieked, terrified by the unfolding scene.

"Under the table!" Layla shouted, the noise from whizzing bullets and broken glass piercing their ears.

She grabbed her frightened daughters and flung them under the table. Romeo was waiting there, too, seemingly dazed by the commotion.

"Mama, what do we do?" Hailey asked. Her voice was shaking, her little body making it flutter.

Bethany was crying too hard to speak.

Layla opened her eyes wide, thinking fast. She wondered who would be here shooting at them and why, but those questions had to remain in the background. She'd need to react in a way that would save her girls. She wished she knew exactly what to do. She couldn't tell Hailey that she didn't know.

"Cover your heads," Layla said. "Like this."

She laced her fingers together and showed the girls how to do the same. They cried as they followed directions.

In the next room, Mikhail had gotten a gun from somewhere and was returning fire through the now open windows. He hid behind the heavy front door, popping out to take aim each time the gunfire from the front yard slowed.

"Get out of here!" he shouted to Layla and the girls. "Go!"

"Where?" Layla asked.

She couldn't send the girls to their rooms to wait for a code word when the house was being shot up. She needed to keep them with her. She couldn't exactly run out the back door, either. What if the house was surrounded?

Layla was aware that anything she and Mikhail said to each other could be heard by the gunmen outside. Her mind felt scrambled, but that much was clear.

"Basement!" Mikhail called between rounds. "Barricade yourselves inside and don't open up for anyone."

"Right," Layla mumbled.

She knew he was right. It was the only option.

Luckily, the door to the basement was adjacent to the kitchen. Layla and the girls would only need to make it across an open expanse of about six feet to reach it. If they stayed low and crawled, there was a good chance they'd make it. Romeo might follow them to safety, too.

"Okay, girls," she began, "the three of us are going to crawl to the basement door. We'll go downstairs to hide until more help gets here. Do you understand?"

Gunfire continued and more glass shattered, this time from the back of the house. Layla's suspicion had been correct. They were surrounded. The basement was the only option. And they were running out of time.

"We have to move fast," Layla said.

Bethany hid her head and continued to cry. It was heartbreaking to see the girls so afraid. Layla was afraid, too. Very afraid. Perhaps even more afraid than the girls. She couldn't let on.

"I'm going to count to three," Layla said. "When you hear me say three, we crawl as fast as we can to the basement door. Okay?"

They nodded through tears, their wet faces hurting Layla's heart.

"Hailey, you go first. Then you, Bethany. I'll go last and shut the door behind us," she said.

"What about Micky-Hail?" Bethany pleaded. "He needs to come, too."

"Honey, we have to go without him. I'm sorry," Layla said sadly. "Now, it's time."

Layla reached for her mobile phone on the table top, but couldn't find it right away. A bullet flew so close to her arm that she could feel the breeze. It made every hair on her body stand on end.

That provided the final push. There was no time for a phone, or anything else. They had to go, right that minute.

"Here we go," she said loudly. "One, two… three!"

Layla gave Hailey a push and she crawled as instructed, her little arms and legs moving as fast as they could. Bethany followed, moving a bit slower. Layla brought up the rear.

They scrambled despite the chaos around them. Romeo followed, too, reaching Hailey just as she turned the knob to open the basement door. In a series of deliberate movements, Layla successfully got them all behind the door. She locked the hand lock and fastened a chain on the top. She knew that wouldn't hold the gunmen off for long, though.

"Follow me," she said as she led the girls down the narrow stairs.

She'd have to take them to a part of the house they'd never seen before. A part that she and Trent had outfitted a long time ago for just such an occasion.

18

LAST WORDS

For two whole days, Layla stayed in the Grant family's underground bunker with the girls and Romeo. By this time, it had been a full week since Ivan and his strange vehicle had pulled into the driveway and wreaked havoc on their previously idyllic existence.

In retrospect, Layla wished she and Trent had been more proactive in handling the danger that was to come. They'd waited, like sitting ducks.

They should have known that the Russian government would send people to punish them for Trent's carelessness in getting himself accused of bank fraud. Because that's what this had to be. Layla couldn't imagine another explanation for what had happened.

Layla and Trent had both heard stories of untimely ends for Russian agents who had tried to escape their country's rule. Most often, those agents were poisoned, fated to turn up dead under mysterious circumstances.

When asked, Russian leader Vladimir Putin never admitted to any involvement in those agents' deaths. Yet he always made comments about how treason was an unforgivable offense against the motherland.

Putin was a vengeful man who believed that traitors must be punished. Layla knew he'd order her killed if he even suspected she was disloyal. That made Layla wonder if Russia had ordered that Mikhail be killed as well. Had he been too friendly? Too soft on her and the girls? It saddened her deeply to think that Mikhail had put himself in harm's way for her family. She wished she knew what had happened to him, but she hadn't dared to leave the bunker until she was absolutely sure it was safe.

There was a sad irony to the fact that Rosemary Run was such a quiet, peaceful small town. The people who lived here probably never thought they'd see this kind of international drama in their own backyards.

Interestingly to Layla, no one had ever suspected the Grant family of being sleeper agents, as far as she knew. That fact was a blessing and a curse now, though, because she had kept to herself so much that it might take a while for someone to realize something was amiss.

There were no neighbors within guaranteed earshot. No one that Layla saw on a regular basis during the summer to notice that they hadn't bumped into her lately. As far as she could tell, if Mikhail had been killed, Fred or Bea were the only people who might check in. Trent was surely too busy romancing Tabby to do anything about his own family's disappearance.

The thought made Layla sick. Even after everything, she was still broken-hearted about her husband's behavior. She hadn't seen it coming.

Exhausted and tired of staying underground, Layla was beginning to go stir crazy.

She and the girls were tired, dirty, and ready to receive help. They'd been washing themselves with wet wipes and bottled water, but that wasn't the same as getting clean in a proper bath or shower. Likewise, they'd been eating canned food. It was sustenance, but it was a far cry from the restaurant dinner at Honey Hog they'd been looking forward to. They'd even been bagging Romeo's seemingly endless piles of poop. What Layla wouldn't have given to simply let the dog out in the backyard like she used to.

"Girls?" Layla began.

Hailey was stretched out on a cot, one leg bouncing over the side. She was a child. Even while hiding out in an underground bunker, she was teeming with energy. Bethany was on a second cot, still groggy from sleep but listening.

"Yes, Mama?" Hailey asked.

"I think it's time for me to go upstairs and get us some help. We've been down here a long time. I haven't heard any movement up there for a long time, either."

"No!" Bethany said, sitting upright. "Mama, stay here. You can't go."

Hailey nodded her agreement.

"I know it's scary," Layla replied, "but I have to go. If I don't, it might be a very long time until someone comes to find us."

"We can wait," Hailey said, clearly traumatized by the violent scene that had occurred when they were last in the main part of the house. "I don't want you to get hurt, Mama. Please stay. Daddy will be back from his work trip soon. Won't he? And Aunt Tabby will come to check on us soon."

Layla still hadn't told the girls about their dad. Not about his upcoming court appearance or about his tryst with Tabby.

"I don't know," Layla said honestly. "I want to go and look around, though. I'm pretty sure it's safe. I doubt those bad guys have been waiting for us all this time. I need to get to a phone so I can call the police."

She'd debated whether or not to involve the police over the prior two days, and had ultimately decided they probably needed to be called. Depending on what she found upstairs, of course.

"Please, Mama," Hailey tried again.

"Honey, you will be okay down here. I wouldn't leave you if I didn't think it was safe," Layla said.

Layla hoped that if she taught the girls to operate the door, they would be okay.

The door to the bunker was steel. The whole thing was expansive, designed to withstand an apocalypse-- earthquake, flood, nuclear blast, and more. There was enough food and supplies to last a year. In theory, they could survive down here without her, should she meet an untimely end or be whisked away to serve time in a Russian prison.

She had to go above ground. It was time.

"I'm going," Layla reiterated.

Hailey and Bethany nodded reluctantly, fear alight in their eyes. The poor little dears. But it had to be done.

Layla showed them how to open and close the door, then made sure they understood how to get themselves food and other necessities. When she was satisfied that they could handle themselves at a basic level, she exited the bunker cautiously, leaving Romeo behind to, hopefully, provide some measure of additional comfort and protection.

"Stay safe, my little loves," she said quietly as the door closed and sealed behind her.

With that bit of emotional business finished, Layla steeled herself for the task at hand. As she climbed the wooden stairs from the basement to the main level, her heart raced. She had no idea what she'd find up there. No idea what horrors would await.

Her hand trembled as she unlatched the chain and unlocked the handle on the door leading to the kitchen. She paused for a moment, gathering her nerve, then forged ahead, opening the door with one swift movement.

The first thing Layla noticed was that it was a bright, sunny day outside. Birds were chirping loudly as if to insist that life go on, despite the damage sustained. She knew this because most of the glass had come out of the windows, letting the outside in.

As she watched in disbelief, a sparrow flew right into the kitchen and perched on top of a bar stool near where Layla was standing. It tilted its head rapidly from side to side, peering at her.

"Hello, little bird," she whispered. "Are you enjoying my house?" The creature continued to look at her curiously. "I hope so," she continued. "Someone might as well. I've been stuck underground for two days. Two!"

Turning her attention away from the bird, she surveyed the room for something she could use as a weapon. She hadn't accessed the cache of guns downstairs. The weapons were housed in a locked compartment inside the bunker. One that she didn't want the girls to know how to get into. She'd decided it was better to leave those weapons alone unless she absolutely had to.

The decision to scrounge for a makeshift weapon instead of getting a gun out of the cache showed Layla just how different her life was now than when she and Trent had first moved in and stocked the bunker. Back then, she wouldn't have hesitated to arm herself with as many guns as she could get her hands on. Now, though, she was most concerned about the long-term effects on Hailey and Bethany as a result of the things they were exposed to and the trauma they endured.

With her children's wellbeing as priority number one, Layla truly was a new person. A more evolved, honest person. If only she could untangle her life circumstances in order for that to be true at all levels.

"This will work," she mumbled to herself and the little bird as she pulled a heavy lamp from a counter in the kitchen and removed the shade.

Moving slowly and as quietly as possible, Layla maneuvered around the debris on the floor, through broken glass and puddles of water. She wasn't sure where the water had come from. Maybe it had rained?

The house was trashed. It was sad to see. Layla and Trent had decorated the place with meaningful objects chosen carefully and lovingly to make a warm home for their family. Looking around, Layla thought that most of their possessions were a complete loss. Perhaps the things on the second floor had fared better. The main floor was in shambles.

So far, she didn't hear or see evidence of anyone still there. Other than the woodland creatures and their outdoor sounds, the place was quiet.

Unsure where her mobile phone had ended up and so deciding that she'd call the police on the landline phone, Layla worked her way through the dining room and into the living room. She was determined to get the call placed quickly. Even though it seemed like no one was around, she didn't want to waste any time getting help.

"Here goes nothing," she said under her breath as she darted the final distance to the easy chair and the telephone, hopping over more debris along the way.

The phone was still on the table and its cord seemed to be plugged into the wall. The receiver was toppled over, but that was an easy fix. It looked like it should still work, assuming no one had cut the lines outside.

As Layla reached the easy chair and the accent table, she quickly glanced around the living room and foyer areas. They were in similar shape as the kitchen and dining room-- trashed, but void of bad guys.

Her breathing heavy with anticipation, she righted the telephone receiver then checked for a dial tone. Thankfully, one was there. She loosened her grip on the lamp long enough to handle the phone. Hopefully, she wouldn't need the lamp for long.

"Help is *finally* on the way," Layla said happily to herself.

She dialed 9-1-1, then waited.

"9-1-1, what is your emergency?" a familiar smooth baritone voice said.

"Officer Rucker? Is that you?" Layla replied.

She knew it was him the second she'd heard his voice. It had somehow been etched into her memory as a result of the terror she was feeling when she'd called for emergency services a week prior. How drastically things had changed since then.

A week ago, she'd been terrified of Mikhail. Little did she know what an ally he'd turn out to be. She wished her friend and ally could be here now. She'd been wondering where he'd gone and if he was okay.

"That's right," the man on the other end of the phone said. "Officer Devonte Rucker. Who is calling?"

"It's Layla Grant," she replied. "1522 Spice Ridge Road in Rosemary Run. I spoke with you a week ago... when I called in then."

Shuffling papers and clicking computer keys could be heard on the other end of the line. "Please hold," Devonte said briskly.

After a few moments, he returned to the line. "Sorry for the delay. I had to dig out my notes," he said. "I took your call last week, but we were informed it was a false alarm. We radioed for the officers to return to the station. None responded." Then, after a pause, "was it a false alarm?"

"I suppose you could say that," Layla replied.

She wasn't sure how to explain. Not quickly, anyway. That would have to be a lengthy explanation.

"Ma'am, do you have an emergency today?"

"I do," she confirmed. "My daughters and I have been

hiding in our basement for two days. Someone-- or ones, I don't know how many of them-- shot at our house. They broke windows and practically destroyed the place."

"Are they still there?" Devonte asked. "Are you in a safe place?"

More keys clicked on the other end of the phone. It sounded like Devonte was typing furiously. Layla supposed that fast typing speeds were an essential part of the job of a police dispatcher. The sound gave her comfort. It promised a swift response. At least, she hoped so.

"I don't know for sure," Layla replied. "I don't see or hear anyone, but I came straight to the phone. I haven't checked around the place."

"Are you or your daughters injured?"

"No, thank God. We're fine."

"Okay, ma'am," Devonte said, "Officers are on their way. I need you to stay on the line with me until they arrive this time. Do you understand?"

"Yes," Layla said.

"Good. It won't be long until you see blue lights. Officers will be there shortly. Stay with me until then, okay?"

"Okay."

As she waited, the receiver against one ear, Layla thought back to the day of the first 9-1-1 call.

She remembered Tabby rushing up the stairs, then taking the phone out of Layla's hand and assuring her that everything would be alright. "Trust me," Tabby had said so self-assuredly that Layla had done just that.

Very little from that day made any sense now. It was as if things had been turned upside down. The people Layla had thought were her trusted loved ones-- Trent and Tabby-- had turned out to be conniving liars. And the person she thought was a dangerous, menacing threat-- Mikhail-- had turned out to be a true friend.

Layla shook her head as she reflected, her gaze suddenly landing on a familiar object in the far edge of her peripheral vision. When her mind processed what she was seeing, her mouth fell open and she dropped the phone, it hurtling toward the ground and twisting about on the end of its cord.

There, sticking out from the doorway of the guest bedroom was Mikhail's boot. It was tipped horizontally and attached to his leg. Neither were moving.

19

STRETCH

What happened next was all a blur for Layla.

Although she had been through the sadness of leaving her parents and extended family behind in Russia and starting over anew, she hadn't ever lost anyone she cared about. Not lost as in the all too permanent way she had lost her friend Mikhail, now.

As her body caught up with the shock that her mind was struggling to process, Layla leapt from her place next to the phone and scrambled into the guest room where Mikhail's body was lying on the floor.

The smell hit her like a freight train. His body had already begun to decompose.

"Oh, my God," she muttered, reeling from both the sight and the smell. "Mikhail!" she cried.

Layla wanted to go to him, to fling herself across his chest and hug him tightly. To beg him to come back to her so that they could be real friends for the rest of their days. But it was too late for any of that.

Mikhail was long gone. He'd been shot multiple times,

the holes in his flesh expanding as they continued to rot. Clearly, he'd been killed the day she and the girls had gone to the basement.

She felt terrible for leaving him up here to die alone. What if she had been able to save him?

Layla spun slowly in circles as she fought to maintain some semblance of composure. Her hand didn't leave her mouth. She was devastated by her discovery, and she didn't know what to do with herself.

Her thoughts jumped from the senselessness of the loss of a precious life to the hurt Ivan would feel when he learned his brother had been killed. Ivan might not have been the best guy, but it had seemed like he and Mikhail cared for each other.

Then suddenly, Layla thought about the ache that Hailey and Bethany would feel when they found out what had happened to their beloved Micky-Hail. She glanced toward the kitchen, praying they'd stay put in the bunker. They certainly didn't need to see-- or smell-- this. Layla wished she'd never seen it herself.

Unable to stand any longer, she dropped to her knees in the hallway outside the door. It was there that the police found her moments later as they entered the Grant family's desecrated home and began to process the scene.

A kind officer of about Layla's age wearing a blue uniform touched her on the shoulder.

Layla's vision had become blurry. Maybe she had passed out. She wasn't sure, but she knew that she was lying down now. The officer's face was friendly. He had dirty blonde hair that was cropped close against the sides of his head.

"Ma'am, are you Layla Grant?" he asked as he used a finger and thumb to check her pulse. "Did you call 9-1-1?" She nodded feebly. "Okay, Layla, I'm Officer James Tatum. We're here to take care of you now. You're going to be alright."

"My daughters…" she said through gritted teeth. Her body seemed to be short circuiting again, only far worse this time than ever before. Her mind was thinking things that she needed to say, but the words were getting jumbled up in her mouth like alphabet soup.

"What's that?" James asked.

"My girls…"

Officer Tatum raised up on his knees and leaned back, calling to another member of his team. It suddenly seemed like the house was full of people. The walls buzzed and the floors hummed with activity.

"Anyone find little girls?" he asked the room. "Vital records say they should be five and seven-years-old. Hailey Grant and Bethany Grant. Are they here?"

Layla shook her head, hoping the motion would shake her out of the fog. It didn't. She remained confused. It felt like the shock of seeing Mikhail's decaying body had caused her conscious mind to disengage to protect her. She'd heard of that happening, but didn't know what it would be like to experience it firsthand.

"No sign of them," someone replied. "Were they supposed to be here?"

James leaned down closer to Layla again. "Are your girls in the house, Layla?"

She nodded feebly. She sputtered and mumbled, but

finally got the words out. "The basement. They're in the basement."

James leaned back again and called out to the team, "Check the basement! She says they're down there."

Layla needed to explain about the bunker and how the girls wouldn't open the door for anyone but her, but her voice continued to fail her.

A thin woman with a black bag and a stethoscope came to listen to Layla's heart and lungs, though Layla didn't pay much attention to what was being done to her. She felt like she was beside her body, not in it. It was the strangest sensation.

As Layla watched from her spot on the floor, a pair of medics came in and placed a stretcher beside Mikhail's body. There was talk of processing the scene and collecting evidence, but they soon rolled him into a black body bag and zipped it all the way to the top, then they hoisted him onto the stretcher and wheeled him outside to an ambulance that was waiting in the driveway.

"He was my friend," she managed.

"What's that?" James asked, apparently unable to hear Layla's quiet voice.

"My friend," she said again, pointing in the direction they had taken Mikhail's body.

"Did you know that man?" James asked.

Layla nodded.

"Can you tell me his name?" James leaned down closer to hear her response, turning his head so that one ear was ready and waiting.

Layla closed her eyes, thinking about Mikhail and how full of life he'd been just a few days before. She could still see him tending to the girl and smiling as they called him Micky-Hail. This was such a tragedy.

"Mikhail Semenov," she said, as loud as she could.

"Michael?" James tried.

Layla bet Mikhail had gotten that a lot.

"No, Mikhail," she said. Then she spelled it out, "M-I-K-H-A-I-L, last name S-E-M-E-N-O-V."

James scribbled the name down on a small notepad he'd pulled from the breast pocket of his shirt. Using the radio receiver on his shoulder, he pressed the button and relayed the information, presumably to dispatch.

If Layla had considered it beforehand, perhaps she wouldn't have given the police Mikhail's real name. She had no idea of the implications for Ivan, or any of the rest of them. As far as she knew, Mikhail was a Russian national and a government agent involved in international espionage. There would be ramifications of him being found dead at the Grant family home.

Unfortunately, though, Layla was too out of sorts to have tried to cover this up. She wasn't sure she would have been capable of doing so, anyway. She wasn't trained for this sort of thing. Not even close.

"Layla," James said, snapping his fingers in front of her face. He'd apparently been trying to get her attention.

"Yeah?" she replied, telling herself to snap out of it.

"We need to find your children. You said they were in the basement, but we haven't been able to find them. Are you certain they're in the house?" he asked.

Layla nodded again as the medic working on her slid a blood pressure cuff over one arm and began to inflate the balloon. Each pump made a swishing sound that seemed to mimic what was happening in Layla's head.

Have I eaten enough? Layla wondered. *Did I pass out from low blood sugar?*

She'd never experienced anything like this. She was struggling to make sense of it.

"They're here," she confirmed. "Hidden in the basement. They're safe."

Suddenly, something fell in the living room, making a loud crashing sound. Layla jumped and shook so violently that the woman taking her blood pressure jerked back.

"What was that?" Layla asked. "Is someone here?"

Her mind immediately went to the worst-case scenario as visions of hostile shooters filled her thoughts. It didn't seem too far-fetched to imagine that they were back. Perhaps they'd been waiting for signs of activity at the house. If the shooters were Russians sent to punish Layla and Trent, they'd stop at nothing to get the job done.

James put a gentle hand on her shoulder. "Relax," he said. "No one will hurt you while we're here. I promise you that."

Layla could feel the sincerity in his words. She thought James seemed capable. She decided to trust him. What choice did she have?

"Okay," she said, her voice stronger now. The rush of adrenaline had given her strength.

"What about your girls?" James persisted. "We need to find them. To make sure they're okay. They might need medical attention. You say they're hidden in the basement?"

Layla nodded.

"Where?"

"There's a bunker. In the very back behind a curtain. It's built into the wall and hard to see."

James turned and announced this information to his team. Several uniformed officers went to the kitchen, then marched down the stairs to the basement.

"Okay," he said. "We'll get them. They're going to be okay."

Layla shook her head while trying to stand. "I have to go to them. They won't open the door for anyone but me."

James started to stop her, but didn't.

He looked at the medic who had just finished taking Layla's blood pressure. The woman nodded her approval. "She's fine-- physically," the woman said. "Just in shock. Keep her close for a while."

"Got it," he replied as he helped Layla get onto her feet. "We'll go downstairs together. We'll get your girls. Okay?"

Layla nodded feebly, then she allowed James to help support her weight. "Where will we go?" she asked as she walked slowly with the officer.

"To get your girls from the bunker in the basement. Remember?"

She shook her head quickly. James thought she was confused. She wasn't. "I mean after. Where will we stay? We can't stay here."

James raised his brows up and down, then nodded, conceding that Layla was right. "We can take you to the hospital and assign a guard to keep watch outside of your door. That's probably the best idea until we get the three of you a clean bill of health. It will also buy us some time to figure out next steps. Forensics will need to thoroughly process your house. It will be a few days before a clean-up crew will be allowed to disturb the scene."

Layla closed her eyes once more and shook her head. "How awful for my little girls. I don't want them to see any of this. I don't want them to have to spend the night in the hospital, then go God knows where."

"I can understand that," James replied. "But you have to, ma'am. Things like this happen. It's a part of life, sad to say."

"Yeah, well, my responsibility as a mother is to protect them from this stuff. To shield them from the harsher realities until they're older and better equipped to handle them."

The pair walked slowly down the steps to the basement. There were a trio of officers already down there, but they moved out of the way to give Layla and James some space.

"Do you have children, James?" Layla asked as they neared the door to the bunker.

She wanted to know if he was capable of understanding just how traumatic this would be for her children. She hoped he was.

"No children of my own, but I have a niece and two nephews. I love those kids dearly, as if they were my own."

"Good," Layla replied, then she called out to the girls and opened the door to the bunker.

PLEAS

Thanks to James and his team of Rosemary Run police officers, Layla and her girls made it out of the house safely. They had been taken to the local hospital where they had been resting comfortably for the past two days. They weren't injured, but they'd been treated for shock and given plenty of fluids as a precaution.

Trent had excellent health insurance benefits through his employer. Layla figured she might as well use them and anything else she could squeeze out of the weasel.

It was day seven since Trent's departure. It was day three since Layla had learned of her husband's betrayal. And it was only day two since the Grant family home had been stormed and Mikhail killed.

Trent was due in court in a few more days, although Layla cared less and less whether he was convicted or not. She had bigger problems to deal with.

Berryhill Community Medical Center was located in the neighboring town of Sweet Balm Bay. It wasn't far from Rosemary Run, but the extra bit of distance gave Layla an added measure of comfort. Maybe the men chasing after her would have a harder time finding her there. Or maybe not. They hadn't found her yet. She was taking it day by day.

James had been a huge help in assisting Layla with making various arrangements. He and his wife, Rebecca, had even taken Romeo in temporarily until Layla got back on her feet. James was due to arrive any minute now with supplies in advance of hospital checkout, including the clothes and shoes Rebecca had purchased for Layla and the girls.

"Hello, hello," James said as he came through the door with several big bags over his arm.

"Hey there," Layla said.

She trusted James and felt comfortable with him, but they still didn't know each other well. Since she had only recently made friends with Mikhail and then lost him, Layla was hesitant to be too chummy too fast. Hailey and Bethany seemed to feel the same.

The girls were in reasonably good spirits, although they sat and stared a lot. They kept asking Layla where Daddy and Aunt Tabby were and why they couldn't see either of them. Layla had finally broken down and tried to call Trent from the hospital phone, but she hadn't been able to get through. It had seemed that his number was disconnected.

"I have bagels and juice," James said. 'And clothes. I hope you ladies like everything."

It was mid-morning and dreary outside. The rainy weather seemed to match Layla's mood.

"Thank you," Layla said as she took the food from James and began to spread it out on a rolling tray table for the girls.

It was pitiful how far they had fallen in such a short amount of time. It reminded Layla of her humble beginnings in Russia, rubbing elbows with her siblings because there wasn't enough room to spread out.

Layla took a deep breath and forced herself to focus on the positive though. She and the girls were healthy, and they were all safe for now. As a bonus, she had the hope that Fred might still be working with United States government officials who might help her to defect to this country for a chance to live in peace with her children. She knew it was a long shot, but it was the only shot she had.

"I know it isn't much," James continued, "but Rebecca and I tried to pick out clothes like the ones we saw you wearing in pictures."

"You have pictures of us?" Layla asked, suddenly feeling defensive.

James backtracked quickly. "On Facebook," he said. "The ones you'd posted publicly."

"Oh," Layla said. "That makes sense."

The girls had tensed when Layla had. They were all jumpy. Afraid to trust completely. Layla wondered if they could ever go back to the way they once were.

"That's very kind of you, and Rebecca," she replied.

"We're happy to help," he said sincerely. "Truly, we are."

Layla picked at her bagel, still too numb to eat much.

"I brought you a new phone," James added. "A burner.

You can just ditch it when you have a chance to visit your carrier and get a better one. Donate this one to the station, maybe? They're always looking for extra devices to give to people in need."

Layla took the phone from his hands and nodded. "I'll do that. Thanks again."

"And I know you'll need a car," James said. "Your van was towed to impound. I'm afraid it isn't driveable."

The girls looked especially sad to hear this, but they were becoming jaded by now. They kept chewing, their appetites better than their mother's.

"I guess we will," Layla confirmed. "We have money. That isn't a problem. It's just the time to make the arrangements."

"I know," James said. "There will be time for all of that. But there are things you need right now. Believe me, I've seen situations like this before. It's an unfortunate part of my job."

"Sounds like it," Layla said. "I'm sorry."

James nodded slowly. "No need to be sorry. I knew what I was getting myself into. You, on the other hand, did not. That's why I feel so strongly about helping you. It's no trouble at all."

Layla winced as his words settled over her. She had known what she was getting herself into when she signed up to be a Russian sleeper agent. She *should* have, anyway. She couldn't help but wonder if James would be so kind if learned that truth.

Maybe it was because of everything she had lost, but Layla suddenly wanted to tell James the whole truth. She wanted to tell the girls the truth, too. About her background, her desire to become a real American, all of it. The urge to come clean was overwhelming. She didn't think she could hold it in if she tried.

If the three of them were to survive, the girls would have to know. Surely, even Mikhail would agree with that statement given what they were facing. They were essentially homeless right now. And really bad guys were after them. And Trent had, apparently, abandoned them for other pursuits.

Layla decided right then and there. It was time to put her faith in the Americans who could help her. And it was time to let the girls see her do it.

She was tired of pretending. Tired of hiding in plain sight, and with no desire to hide out of sight any more than they already had in the bunker. At least, not without the protection of the American government.

"James?" Layla asked.

Her tone was low, serious. James and the girls took notice.

"Yeah?"

"I have something important to tell you."

James lowered his brow and put on his police officer face. Layla could tell he was instantly conflicted as to how he should handle whatever she was going to say. James was a good, honorable, honest officer. That was plain to see.

"Will this be a confession?" he asked, his tone equally serious.

The girls looked at each other, worry in their eyes. Layla noticed and pulled them close to her. The three of them huddled together on the hospital bed, arms around each other.

"Don't be afraid, girls. Be brave. I want you to hear what I'm going to say. Okay?"

They nodded. Layla pushed on, gaining strength from the prospect of living a life of integrity. Somehow. Some way.

Layla turned her attention back to James. "It's part confession, part plea for help."

He stiffened, sitting upright in his chair. "So you know," he began, "I have a duty to report…"

She stopped him. "I know. Just listen. Please. I-- we-- need your help."

He paused for what felt like a long time as he rubbed a spot on his temple with one thumb. Finally, he nodded and raised a hand, motioning for Layla to go on.

"What I'm about to say will be hard to believe at first, but it's the truth. I promise. I'll provide all the proof you need once the girls and I are somewhere safe."

"Okay," James replied. "I can't guarantee…"

"*Listen*," Layla said.

"Okay."

Layla took the biggest, deepest breath she could hold. She glanced out the window at the rain that had formed beads on the glass. The sound of its drip, drip soothed her and provided the courage she needed to speak her truth.

"My real name is Petra Ozlov. My husband's name is Dmitriy Kozlov. We're from Russia."

Hailey's eyes grew as wide as saucers. "That's what Mikhail called you, the first day he came to our house. Petra. You said he wasn't telling the truth."

Layla smoothed the hair on the top of Hailey's little head. "I know, honey, and I'm sorry for not telling you the truth right then and there. In fact, I'm sorry for not telling you the truth all along. It's your heritage, too. You have a right to know."

"Mama, what is heritage?" Bethany asked. She wasn't catching on as easily as Hailey.

"It's the culture where your family comes from," Layla explained. The little girl nodded, happy with that much explanation, for now.

"We're from Russia?" Hailey asked.

"Daddy and I are, so you are, too," Layla replied.

"Do we have a grandpa and grandma in Russia?" Hailey tried.

She had often asked why kids at school had extended family members that the Grant girls didn't. Hailey was at the age where differences between kids stood out in her mind.

"You do!" Layla answered. "And you have aunts and uncles and cousins."

James laced his fingers together and placed them behind his head. He was struggling with how to handle this, and his body was showing signs of his distress. He wasn't picking up his phone or leaving the room yet, so that much was good.

"Trent and I agreed to be sleeper agents working for the Russian government," Layla continued. "I can't speak for Trent since he isn't here right now, but as for myself, I was young and didn't understand what I was getting into."

James lowered his hands and squinted his eyes.

"I went through very little training. Just some classes that were more propaganda than anything else. Trent and I hadn't been married long, and we were recruited to come to the United States and act like a normal married couple. We'd already learned to speak English in school, so when we got here, we blended in quickly and easily. Trent was sent to college and graduate school, paving the way for his successful career in the banking industry. I was told to focus on being a normal housewife and mother."

For the first time since hearing this bombshell, James spoke. "But you said you are a sleeper agent. Meant to be activated when the time is right and you're needed by your government."

"Yes," Layla confirmed. "Again, I can't speak for Trent right now, but I don't want to do that anymore. I want to keep my girls safe. I want to become a real American."

"So, you're telling me you want to defect to the United States," James said.

Layla nodded enthusiastically.

"Is sleeping your job?" Hailey asked, trying to sort through the information.

Layla chucked. It felt good to be getting this off her chest. She already felt lighter, more free. It was as if a lead weight had been lifted. Mikhail would have wanted it that way.

"No, honey, not exactly. I'll explain it to you later. For now, just know that I want my job to be taking care of you and Bethany without any secret job in the background. Whatever it takes to make that happen, I'll do."

Then Layla proceeded to tell James the whole story, beginning to end. He stayed, and he listened.

JUSTICE IS SERVED

The Day of the Sentencing

L ayla was angry. Urgently, desperately angry.

The prior two weeks had seen her make and lose a dear friend, get shot at and have to hide underground with her poor little girls, learn that her husband was cheating on her with her best friend, and be forced to fend for herself as she begged U.S. government officials to help her start a new life.

To say the least, it had been one hell of a time. The most tumultuous and terrifying of Layla's entire life.

Her blood boiled inside her veins. Since she had learned that the only way to make a deal with the United States would be to enter witness protection, she'd tried literally every possible way to stuff her anger down, to wish it away, to numb it, to drown it with alcohol, and even to take it out on others who might help shoulder the burden.

Nothing had worked. She'd remained imprisoned by her rage.

It seemed there was no escape. Not for Layla or for Trent, who was facing serious federal charges that could land him in prison for up to thirty years. Not to mention, he could be fined as much as one million dollars. Those facts only stoked the fires of Layla's anger ever further, her organs feeling like molten lava that would soon melt and burn her from the inside out.

How dare he betray me and then leave me? she thought.

Trent would go away to prison and then Layla would go away with the girls into witness protection. They'd never be able to speak to each other again. Never able to reconcile. From this point forward, the girls would not know their father.

Layla smoothed her hair nervously as she waited with the crowd that had gathered in the courtroom for Trent's sentencing. People scurried down the main walkway to find a seat on one of the crowded wooden benches, hoping to get settled into a spot before the room was called to order.

A jury had found Trent guilty of bank fraud just two days earlier, and the judicial system had seemed keen to dole out the broken man's punishment as soon as humanly possible. Other than a few quick glances across the courtroom a couple of days prior, Layla had not seen or spoken to her husband since he'd left with Ivan Semenov in the strange, angular vehicle.

Despite Layla's wish for space and privacy, a balding

old man in a tweed jacket sat down beside her. She gave him a quick smile, but wasn't in any frame of mind to chat. She was afraid that if she opened her mouth to speak to the man, her vitriol would spill out. So, she kept her gaze facing forward, focusing on the back of her husband's head as she tapped a fingertip nervously on one knee.

Tears stung at Layla's eyes. She tried desperately to force them away.

She could usually hide her emotions. She'd had years of practice in pretending that everything was alright. But today, doing so seemed harder than ever. The proceedings seemed so life-changing. So final.

Layla hoped she could hold it together for the entirety of the proceedings. Fred had warned her that a dramatic display of emotion could irritate the judge and make him come down harder on Trent as a result. Even though she was angry with her husband, she didn't wish more prison time on him. She wasn't a monster. And besides, Fred had been the key in securing Layla's deal with the U.S. government. She owed him the courtesy of doing what he asked.

Once things got started, time moved at what felt like warp speed, everything set on fast forward. The crowd stood as Judge Trumbell entered, then flattened his silky black robe, got comfortable behind the bench, and pounded his gavel. When he was finished, the people in the courtroom went back down as shuffling and nervous energy permeated the space.

There had been a lot of media interest in Trent's case. Judge Trumbell had barred members of the media from entering the courtroom, but a gaggle of reporters and cameramen waited anxiously outside to report on today's outcome the minute they received the news.

Just a short time prior, no one in Rosemary Run had known about the charges. But like a beachball stuffed under the surface of water, there would be no hiding the truth. Just as that beachball would eventually bounce upward, forcing its way out and into the open air, the truth of the Grant family's predicament had found its way into the light of day.

One benefit of the two weeks from hell was that Layla no longer cared what townspeople thought. Several of them who had learned about her family's woes had been kind-- like Bea and James.

It had probably helped that one of Trent's co-workers at the bank, Moe Griffith, was facing similar charges as an alleged co-conspirator. Fred wasn't representing Moe, but he had advised Layla that once Moe went before a federal judge next week, it should take most of the attention off of the Grants.

Moe was a former NFL football player, making the pending charges against him all the more scandalous. Also helpful was the fact that the public believed Trent was a regular guy. No one had uncovered the deeper truth.

Layla's palms sweat as she wrung her hands, feeling the hardness of the unforgiving bench beneath her.

Luckily, she could focus on what was happening without having to tend to her two young girls at the same time. Hailey and Bethany had stayed home with their aunt, Tabatha Rhodes, affectionately called Aunt Tabby. Tabby had recently retired from her decades-long job as a school bus driver, and she was happy to find things to fill her newfound free time.

It had pained Layla to communicate with Tabby, but James had advised her to let the girls see the woman before they went into witness protection. He had said it was a small kindness for children who had few close connections to begin with. Layla had agreed. While she was still angry at Tabby, too, she trusted her to take good care of Hailey and Bethany while their parents were in court.

The trouble Trent faced was more than the Grant girls could comprehend. In fact, Layla had insisted that no one tell the girls the truth of what was really happening. If Trent did-- *God forbid*-- get sent to prison, Layla would tell the girls that he was away traveling for work. She knew it sounded preposterous because their father's sentence could span decades, but protecting her family was priority number one. The girls wouldn't have been able to contact their father from witness protection, anyway, and they'd already had to absorb enough when they'd learned that their parents were sleeper agents from Russia.

In a whirlwind of activity, the courtroom participants followed instructions and routine until it was time for Judge Trumbell to speak the words that would likely change the course of Trent's life forever. Those words would affect his family, too. In a big way.

Layla thought her husband looked weak and frail standing there, bright overhead lights shining hotly on his head of thinning brown hair. He squinted and pursed his lips like a cave-dwelling creature who hadn't seen the light of day in some time.

The stress had taken a toll on Trent and he'd missed one too many workouts. Love handles bulged from his sides. His hunched back made him look easily fifteen-years older. Gone were the muscle tone and physicality of the athletic man Layla had married a decade prior.

Layla felt a pang of guilt as she contemplated Trent, his softness and vulnerability, in part, her fault. Had she underestimated the stress placed upon him as the sole breadwinner? Had their Russian handlers placed more pressure on him due to his career and corporate connections? Even though she was angry with him, she felt compassion for him, too. She found herself in a strange mental place, unable to feel one emotion without the other.

"Does your client wish to say anything before the sentence is imposed?" the judge finally asked, eyeing Trent's council.

Attorney Fred Lowell stood next to Trent at the defendant's table. Fred was known for representing white collar criminals all over Northern California. His track record was good but that didn't mean he was a miracle worker. He had already advised Trent to expect a hefty fine and a significant amount of prison time.

There was no escaping the need to make amends and restitution.

Trent's voice was small and timid, cracking like a teenage boy's as he replied. "No, your honor."

Judge Trumbell spoke quickly, his words booming throughout the room.

"Then I hereby sentence you to a term of twenty-nine

years in federal prison and a fine of nine-hundred-and-fifty-thousand-dollars. Court is adjourned."

The courtroom erupted into a sea of murmurs, gasps, and a few claps upon hearing the news. Someone ran out the back door, presumably to share details with members of the media. Within minutes, Trent's fate would be heard far and wide on TV newscasts and in newspaper articles. Not many minutes later, Layla would be whisked away to pick up the girls and then to be taken to their new home in their new city, where they would get new names and identities.

Layla thought she saw her husband's knees buckle, and hers threatened to do the same.

She wanted to scream. Every fiber of her being wanted to wail like a banshee, to let out the frustration and the rage that had consumed her once tranquil existence.

Her fists curled into tight balls. She wanted to pound the marble column in front of her and have it give like bread dough. She wanted the column to bend and bulge inward, taking her pain with it. Her pain needed somewhere to go. If not the column, she wanted to turn and rip the wooden benches from the floor like the Incredible Hulk, busting bolts and loosening screws with ease. She wanted to smash and destroy everything in her sight. She wanted to crush the things around her in the hopes that doing so might dampen the fury pouring from her soul.

But she couldn't.

Countless eyes were on Layla, watching for a reaction, gauging her handling of the news. She'd be a single parent soon, left to raise the girls and manage her single-parent family's affairs on her own.

Layla hadn't worked outside of the home since she'd become pregnant with Hailey eight years prior. Even then, she had been a low-rate retail manager with income too meager to provide for a family. She had let Trent, an MBA grad, be the breadwinner and handle their finances. Even though Layla's employment prospects didn't look good, she had been told that she'd have a new job to go along with her new life in witness protection. She wondered what it would be and if she'd enjoy it.

As she stared at the scene in front of her, her husband a shell of the man she once knew who was destined to spend the better part of the rest of his life behind bars, it took every ounce of Layla's mental fortitude to hold herself together without making the kind of dramatic scene she'd been warned about.

Her consciousness was a dense, hot fog of worries and regrets, but a single thought crossed Layla's mind: Her plan had backfired, in a monumental, devastating way.

She had been the one who had schemed with Moe Griffith to embezzle money from the bank to line the Grant family coffers.

She'd had it all planned, until Trent had gotten himself and Moe arrested and then convicted of bank fraud, drawing the attention of their Russian handlers and setting off a chain of events from which there could be no return.

Had Trent somehow known about her torrid affair with Moe and their plan to run away together?

Layla didn't think so. Every indication was that Trent

had remained clueless, a trusting idiot destined to make a royal mess of things.

Layla and her lover had been extra careful to keep their relationship hidden. They had stolen precious moments where they could, while the girls had been at art class or out with their Aunt Tabby.

But now, things were botched. Trent's departure and the events that followed had left Layla no choice but to plead with the Americans to keep her safe.

As she climbed into the back seat of the van that would take her and the girls to the airport for their new life far away from Rosemary Run, Layla thought about how this outcome could only be considered a loss.

She had no Moe, no Trent, no access to money beyond whatever low-wage job she'd be provided, and— most importantly— no chance of ever having total control over her own life.

Had it all been worth it? Petra Ozlov thought not.

THE END.

———

Get the next book in the series:

Her Every Breath
Rosemary Run - Book Nine

———

Want to connect with Kelly?

Sign up for her email newsletter at kellyutt.com and never miss a deal or new release.

ENJOY THIS BOOK?

A NOTE FROM AUTHOR KELLY UTT

Did you enjoy this book? You can make a big difference.

Honest reviews of my books help bring them to the attention of other readers.

If you've enjoyed this book, I would be very grateful if you could spend just five minutes leaving a review (it can be as short as you like) on the book's retail page where you purchased and on Goodreads or BookBub.

Thank you very much.

ABOUT THE AUTHOR

STANDARDS OF STARLIGHT BOOKS
KELLY UTT

Kelly Utt writes emotional, pulse-pounding domestic suspense novels with characters who show up for each other when it counts. She was born in Youngstown, Ohio in 1976.

Kelly grew up with a dad who would read a book on a weighty topic, ask her to read it, too, and then insist they discuss it together, igniting her passion for life's big questions. That passion is often reflected inKelly's novels, giving them a depth which leaves readers wanting more and thinking about her stories long after the last lines are read.

Kelly holds a Bachelor's degree in psychology from the University of Tennessee, Knoxville and she studied graduate-level interactive media and communications at Quinnipiac University.

She lives in Nashville, Tennessee with her husband and sons. She also writes dark psychological thrillers with one of her sons as the combined pen name Christopher Kelly.

www.kellyutt.com